Texas Grooms Wanted! is a brand-new miniseries in Harlequin Romance®.

Meet three wonderful heroines who are all looking for very special Texas men—their future husbands!

Good men may be hard to find, but these women have experts on hand. They've all signed up with the Yellow Rose Matchmakers. The oldest—and the best!—matchmaking service in San Antonio, Texas, the Yellow Rose guarantees to find any woman her perfect partner....

So, for the cutest cowboys in the whole state of Texas, read:

Only cowboys need apply…

Books in this series are:

HAND-PICKED HUSBAND by
Heather MacAllister in January 1999
BACHELOR AVAILABLE! by Ruth Jean Dale
in February 1999
THE NINE-DOLLAR DADDY by Day Leclaire
in March 1999

Name: Ruth Jean Dale

Age: 39 and holding…

Occupation: Romance author

Marital status: Married, one of the few things I managed to get right the first time around.

Ideal partner: The one I've got. He may be the only man in the Western world able to put up with my eccentricities—and I happily return the favor.

Worst dating experience: So long ago I don't even remember, although I do recall I kissed a few frogs before finding my prince. Fortunately, all you need is one if he's the *right* one! I guess that's why I write romance—because I found my own happy ending was just the beginning.

Bachelor
Available!
Ruth Jean Dale

TEXAS
GROOMS
WANTED!

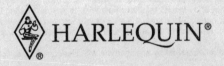

TORONTO • NEW YORK • LONDON
AMSTERDAM • PARIS • SYDNEY • HAMBURG
STOCKHOLM • ATHENS • TOKYO • MILAN • MADRID
PRAGUE • WARSAW • BUDAPEST • AUCKLAND

For Day Leclaire,
who roamed San Antonio and the Hill Country of Texas
with me to research this book
(and hers).
If you've got bulls to herd, Day's your cowgal!

ISBN 0-373-03539-X

BACHELOR AVAILABLE!

First North American Publication 1999.

Copyright © 1998 by Betty Lee Duran.

Printed in U.S.A.

CHAPTER ONE

From: SuperScribe@BoyHowdy.com
Sent: Sunday, Nov. 1, 9:42 p.m.
To: MataHari@Upzydazy.com
Subject: Enough, already!
Okay, Emily, I've been patient but I know you and if
you don't hustle your buns over to the Yellow Rose
ASAP, you never will. A promise is a promise (not
that you owe me or anything). :-) (Smile) What's your
problem? You *could* get lucky....

THE first thing that caught Emily Kirkwood's attention Monday when she entered Yellow Rose
Matchmakers in San Antonio, Texas, was the fragrance of roses.

The second thing that caught her attention was the
best-looking cowboy in the world.

One of those two things stopped her in her tracks.
She preferred to think it was the perfumed air, since
she wasn't the kind of woman who let superficial
things like *looks* get to her. She prided herself on dig-
ging deeper for such attributes as honor, integrity,
honesty.

Of course, she couldn't *see* those things at a glance,
while she *could* see curly black hair and lively blue
eyes, long, denim-clad legs and broad shoulders beneath a red plaid shirt. She could also see the spark

of interest that leaped into those incredible eyes, quickly muted when he turned to the receptionist.

"I'm Cody James," he said with a good old Texas drawl, giving the receptionist a sparkling smile. He turned a white cowboy hat between big, competent hands. "I have an eleven o'clock appointment with Wanda Roland but I'm a few minutes early. I'll just take a seat and wait until—"

"Oh, no, Mr. James!" The receptionist appeared to be as impressed with his good looks as Emily was trying not to be. "Wanda's expecting you. Please go right on in." She pointed toward a door.

"Thank you, ma'am." Nodding respectfully, he ambled to the door, knocked lightly and entered.

For a few seconds, both the receptionist and Emily held their collective breaths.

The receptionist, a pretty middle-aged woman whose desk plaque said simply Teresa, fanned herself. "Oh, dear," she said. "I could go for that myself."

Emily laughed politely. "Are all the Yellow Rose clients that good-looking?" She tried to keep the critical note in her voice under control. In her experience, men who were that good-looking were not to be trusted. They were almost as untrustworthy as the rich ones—and rich and handsome was the most dangerous combination in the world. Poor but honest, attractive but not drop-dead gorgeous: those were the only men she was ever going to trust again.

Not that it mattered in this particular instance. She hadn't come to Yellow Rose Matchmakers to find true love but rather to ferret out information for her cousin Terry's magazine article. Research, he'd called it, simple research.

In her more honest moments, she called it spying.

She'd already done similar "research" for him in Dallas before she'd been temporarily transferred to San Antonio by her employer, A&B Construction Company, to help open a new office. The Dallas caper had involved nothing more than filling out a form, making an excruciatingly embarrassing videotape and being matched with a computer geek for a single date. Then she'd written a "dating diary" for Terry and considered the matter closed.

Funny how that first experience had turned out, though. She'd answered every question with total honesty, to no avail—not that she'd actually been looking for a man, she reminded herself. She was simply paying back an old debt of honor to her cousin, nothing more. She certainly wasn't looking for any kind of relationship, permanent or otherwise. At twenty-five, she wasn't sure she'd ever want to get married after seeing all that her parents had put each other through. Being dumped practically at the altar herself hadn't exactly raised men in her esteem, either.

Teresa tapped her pencil on the desktop, her smile friendly and welcoming. "And how may I help you, Ms....?"

"Emily Kirkwood," she responded, belatedly realizing that there must be some kind of mistake. "I also had an eleven o'clock appointment with Ms. Roland. I don't mind coming back at another time, though." Actually, she'd be delighted. She edged toward the door. Terry couldn't blame her for this mixup...could he?

Teresa frowned. "Oh, dear. Has Wanda done it again?" She raised a hand obviously meant to arrest

Emily's flight, lifted the telephone receiver with the other and punched in three numbers. "Please wait while I— Wanda? I'm afraid there's been another mix-up. Emily Kirkwood is here and says she has an— But Mr. James just went in, so I naturally assumed— Oh, all right. Of course." Teresa hung up the phone. "She'll be right out."

Emily, feeling reprieve slipping from her grasp, stared longingly at the front door. "Really, I don't mind coming back. This isn't actually a very good day for me anyway. Maybe..."

The door through which the handsome cowboy had vanished moments earlier opened and a woman bustled through. Emily stopped trying to escape and stared.

Wanda Roland looked like the fairy godmother in a Walt Disney movie. Her snowy white hair might indicate advanced years, but her cheerful, unlined face made her look much younger.

Her smile made her look beautiful. She came forward with hands outstretched. "My dear, I'm so very sorry about the confusion."

"That's quite all right. As I was telling Teresa—"

"And she passed on your concerns, please be assured. We're very much on the ball here at the Yellow Rose." Eyes a paler blue than the handsome cowboy's twinkled beneath snowy brows. "Please, won't you come into my office?"

Emily resisted the tug on her hands. "But there's already someone in there," she demurred. "I don't really think it would be a good idea—"

Wanda laughed, a silvery, tinkling sound. "All my ideas are good ones, dear. You'll see. It's quite a large office with plenty of room for two clients at the same time. Besides, all you'll be doing is filling out forms.'' She made a face as if she found that activity particularly distasteful.

''No, really—''

Wanda slipped an arm like a band of steel around Emily's waist. ''She's shy,'' she informed Teresa. ''Come along, dear. I know what's best.''

Emily had little choice but to ''come along'', guided by the little woman's surprisingly strong grip. Well, why not? she consoled herself. The sooner she got this over with, the sooner she could get on with her life. She certainly wouldn't be sorry to get out from under this sense of obligation to her cousin.

They entered the office and the handsome cowboy looked up, holding a single long-stemmed yellow rose loosely in his hands. When he saw them, he replaced the posy in the bud vase next to his hat, resting brim up on the desktop. Dark brows rose in question but he said nothing.

Wanda didn't seem to be one to let any silence remain unfilled. ''Mr. James—may we call you Cody?—this is Miss Emily Kirkwood. May we call you Emily?''

''Of course,'' they said in unison.

Wanda led Emily to a chair only a couple of feet from Cody's, deposited her there and bustled over to her desk. She had to roll her chair to one side in order to see around the enormous computer that covered the entire right-hand side of the desk's surface. ''Now that we're all here,'' she said with satisfaction, ''we can get to know each other a little better. Don't y'all think that would be nice?''

"Uhh…" Cody James cast an oblique glance at the woman sitting to his left. "Is this how you handle all your new…uh, clients?"

Wanda's frown would have looked like a smile on any other face. "Well, no, not actually. The two of you are a special case, I guess you could say."

Emily leaned forward. "I feel very uncomfortable about this." She turned so she could see the cowboy, who also looked ill at ease. "I don't want to take up Mr. James's time with my—"

"Cody," he said quickly. "I don't mind, Ms. Kirkwood. I'm just confused."

She nodded. "All right, Cody. I'm Emily, and I'm at least as confused as you are."

"See how well we're getting on!" Wanda interjected.

Emily persevered. "Yes, but I still feel like an intruder. Why don't I come back another day?"

Cody's long-lashed blue eyes flew wide. "I'd hate to see you go to that trouble. Look, we had the same appointment, so why don't *I* reschedule? You've got as much right to be here as I do."

"Exactly," Wanda put in quickly. "There's no need for anyone to be inconvenienced."

"But—" they began, in unison again.

"Tut-tut," she said, waving aside their apprehensions. "Look at it this way—you'll be doing me a favor. I'll only have to go through the Yellow Rose spiel—pardon me, the orientation—once instead of twice." She gave a delicate little cough, covered by one soft hand.

Emily looked at Cody, who looked back at her. She saw the smile start around his lips and move to those remarkable eyes, then found herself smiling in return. It was a kind of silent communication that agreed they'd both stay and see what Wanda Roland was up to.

Satisfied, Wanda nodded briskly. "All right, kiddies, I want you to rest assured that all of us here at Yellow Rose Matchmakers have nothing but your best interests at heart. If we had our way, everyone in Texas would be happily married and sending us birth announcements."

Emily made an exclamation of astonishment before she could stop herself. When the other two looked at her with unveiled curiosity, she rushed to explain herself. "I'm not actually looking for marriage," she said. "I'm new in town and thought it would be nice just to meet a few people."

"That's how it always begins," Wanda said cheerily. "You can't marry 'em until you meet 'em, right, Cody?"

Cody grinned. "Right, Wanda. I, on the other hand, won't settle for anything less than marriage. I'm not getting any younger and I want a houseful of kids while I can still enjoy 'em."

Emily could hardly believe her ears. A man who looked as good as this one certainly didn't need a matchmaker to find women willing to marry him. Something strange was going on here...

Wanda nodded emphatically. "That's the spirit, Cody. I'm sure I can find just the right girl for you. In the meantime, there are a few things my boss insists I tell you."

Now we're getting to the good part, Emily thought. Pay attention! You'll have to pass all this on to Terry.

"Yellow Rose Matchmakers is the oldest personal introduction agency in the city of San Antonio—maybe all of Texas." Wanda's previously warm and friendly tone took on a singsong quality, and she spoke about three times as fast as she had before. Obviously, this was not the favorite part of her job. "We have a phenomenal success rate because we use the newest computers and special software developed just for us." She reached out to give her computer a swift pat, as awkwardly as if she never touched the thing unless required to do so. "This is George," she said. "You can trust him."

George? She'd named her computer *George*? Emily was stunned.

Cody slumped back in his chair, long legs extended until his boots disappeared beneath the edge of the desk. "That's one of the reasons I picked this agency," he said. "I'm a big believer in computers. We use 'em all the time at the ranch. Although..." He frowned thoughtfully. "I don't believe we've named any of 'em."

Wanda nodded approvingly before turning to Emily. "And you, dear—why did you choose the Yellow Rose?"

Because my cousin twisted my arm, she thought. Instead, she said, "I like the name. I love roses and yellow ones are my favorite."

Wanda's smile returned. "What a charming answer." She squared her shoulders. "But to proceed—the Yellow Rose has been uniquely successful in matching couples because we *are* completely computerized. We assess each personality, profile each client and..." She seemed to be running out of steam.

"Uhh…we videotape…I mean, if you like that kind of thing…."

Cody frowned. "I'm not sure I do, if you mean that deal where you sit and talk about yourself to a camera. Too much like an auction, if you ask me. Run tapes, say no to this one, maybe to that one. We're not talking cows here."

"Exactly!" Wanda sparkled like a Christmas tree. "It's the human touch that makes all the difference."

Cody nodded. "Once the information has been analyzed by the computer, I'd agree."

"But—" Emily looked from one to the other, puzzled "—in this day and age, I thought everything about the process was automated and computerized and completely impersonal and scientific."

Wanda gasped. "My word, would you like to live in a world where machines tell you whom to love?"

"Well, no, but—"

Cody cut in. He looked as incensed as Wanda did. "And in a world where people are trotted in and out of the video arena like cows in a sale ring?"

"Well, no, but—" Emily cut *herself* off this time. If Terry was looking for a real up-to-date piece on computer dating, the Yellow Rose apparently wasn't going to be it. On the other hand, his research had already supported Wanda's claim that the Rose had the best success rate of any agency in Texas. That's why he'd been so delighted Emily had been temporarily transferred here. "I stand corrected," she said. "I was just surprised, that's all."

"Well, I guess." Wanda looked mollified. "Now that we understand each other, folks, I think it's time for y'all to fill out our scientific in-depth questionnaire.'' She rummaged in the top left drawer of the desk as she spoke, then the drawer on the right. ''The information you give will be held in the *strictest* confidence, to be shared only when the match is made. We're just trying to establish compatibility characteristics between you and your perfect match. That's what we're after—perfection. If not the next best thing... Ah, here it is.''

She pulled a handful of papers from the drawer and spread them on the desk in an untidy pile, then began pulling out a sheet here, two sheets there, rejecting some, accepting others, putting them together in various stacks.

Emily glanced at Cody and caught him glancing at her. They both looked away quickly. Again, she asked herself why a man who looked like this one had to go to a dating agency to find a woman. All he had to do was walk down the street and they'd follow him home in droves.

''Here we go.'' Wanda offered one pile of papers to each of them, followed by two yellow ballpoint pens bearing a line drawing of a rose. ''Now, the two of you can make yourselves comfortable at the conference table.'' She indicated the table set before three tall windows in the converted Victorian. Glass panes swathed in lace turned muted light and shadow into romantic patterns.

Emily's discomfort returned in a rush. Did she really want to sit across from this man and tell lies, even if only on paper? But Cody was rising obediently while Wanda beamed approval. Emily didn't feel she had any choice but to follow him across the room and sink down in the chair he held for her.

And try to conceal her pleasure that some men still followed the old amenities with such perfect assurance.

Cody stared down at the form on the table before him, trying to concentrate. The first part, at least, was easy: Cody James, 30, male, cowboy. Well, he *was* a cowboy, he thought, easing his conscience. *Income.* He was ready for this one. No way would he tell the truth. Carefully, he wrote, "Enough to get by on with enough left over for a wife and kids, if they're not too extravagant."

That worked.

He read the next inquiry. *Build.* He stifled a smile. Yeah, he built—he'd helped build the hay shed on the Flying J a couple of months ago but he didn't figure that's what they wanted to know.

Dumb question. He'd skip it.

His impatient glance shifted just a tad too much and he found himself looking across the table at Emily Kirkwood. She was bent over the forms with total concentration, and he saw her straight white teeth tugging at that full lower lip. Made his mouth water, just watching.

Too bad about her. He'd liked her right away but he would never get involved with another drop-dead beautiful woman as long as he lived. Unfortunately, Emily *was* beautiful. Gritting his teeth, he went back to the form. *Marital Status*: divorced. *Children*: "No, but I sure want some," he wrote.

Then he came to *Type of Residence* and stopped again. In actual fact, he lived in the big main ranch house at the Flying J with a whole passel of other

Jameses but he sure didn't want that known at this early stage of the game. If he was going to find a woman more interested in him than how many cows and buffalo and acres his family owned, some things were better left unsaid. He wrote, "House," and let it go at that.

Pets. That was easy enough. Dogs, a buffalo. Under *Favorite Animals*, though, he chose horses; *Least Favorite*, cats. *Favorite Sport* was rodeo; *Favorite Nonsporting Activity* was watching rodeo and *Favorite Food* was Tex-Mex.

He heaved a sigh of relief; so far so good. He glanced up again, well pleased with himself. His gaze locked with that of the beautiful brown-eyed blonde sitting across from him. For a moment, he forgot all about the vow made on the heels of his divorce.

No more beautiful women. You just couldn't trust 'em.

With her gaze locked with Cody's, Emily forgot to breathe. Surely it wasn't just his good looks, she thought, a little panicky at the way he made her feel. He'd seemed like a very nice man while the three of them were getting acquainted a few minutes earlier.

She gave him a quick, tentative smile and looked back down at her questionnaire. In Dallas she'd filled out the personal information form with unerring accuracy and gotten a lemon. This time she saw no reason to bare her soul.

Next item, *Children.* She wrote, "Goodness, no!" Actually, she liked children, and if she ever married, she'd certainly want them, but that was years and years in the future. No need to go into any of that.

Pets. Cats, of course; she had two back in the apartment she shared with her old friend, Laurie Billingsley. *Least Favorite Animal* gave her pause for thought since she really liked most animals. Finally, she wrote, "Anything big."

Favorite Nonsporting Activity. If she was being honest, the answer to that would be reading. But who would be interested in a woman who'd give that kind of response? She wrote, "Partying," even though it was a barefaced lie. The answer to *General Interests/ Hobbies* would, in actual fact, be volunteer work. She'd taught children to read back in Dallas and would do so again when she returned. But since truth was not required, she wrote, "Shopping!!" with two exclamation points and an *S* with curlicues.

Her *Favorite Food* was macaroni and cheese, but she wrote, "Vegetarian," because it seemed more sophisticated. Under *A Perfect Date Would Be*, she wrote, "Dinner in a four-star restaurant and dancing," when the truth was closer to "A romantic movie at home before a roaring fire and with a bottle of wine."

Ideal Vacation? "A Caribbean cruise," she wrote extravagantly, even knowing she'd be happier in a cabin in the mountains. *Ideal Partner Would Be…*?

This stopped her cold. She couldn't write, "Poor but honest and loving," which was the truth although she didn't suppose anyone would believe it. So she wrote, "Sophisticated, wealthy, handsome man-about-town." And tried not to lift her gaze to the man seated across from her, a man who certainly appeared to be "poor but honest and loving"—and so handsome that her pulse quickened just looking at him.

She was not here to find a husband, or even a serious relationship! She was here to pay a debt of honor. She lowered her head and forced herself to stare at the next question. *What I'm seeking in a relationship.*

Nothing. She wasn't seeking a darn thing. And once she finished this questionnaire and got away from the appealing Cody James, it wouldn't be so hard to remember that. But since she had to write something, she wrote, "Fun and games!" in great big letters.

No more computer geeks for her!

Ideal Partner Would Be...?

Cody frowned at his questionnaire, wishing he could come up with an easy answer. He wasn't sure what his ideal partner would be but he sure knew what she *wouldn't* be.

She wouldn't be like Jessica.

The thought of his ex-wife sent a familiar shaft of irritation through him. She'd said all the right things—until she had him roped and tied. Then all of a sudden, she didn't want children, she didn't want a boring life on a ranch and, eventually, she didn't want him.

She did want his money and she'd made off with a hefty chunk of it. By then, it had been worth it to Cody to be shed of her. But sometimes he still remembered the things about her that he'd loved, things like a quick laugh, a ready humor, a passionate nature...

And she sure was easy on the eyes....

Blond, brown-eyed, peaches-and-cream skin, a figure that made men drool—actually, Jessica looked a lot like Emily Kirkwood. Jessica knew her power, too, although it took him a little while to realize it. Now, two years after the divorce, he realized that he'd based all his hopes and dreams on what she'd said, not on what she'd done. He'd been wearing blinders, he realized in retrospect. He'd seen her with children and she was completely disinterested; he'd seen her with his family on the Flying J and she'd been standoffish and reluctant to join in.

But all the time she'd been insisting that she loved kids and she loved ranch life and she loved big families and—the biggest lie of all—she loved him. He figured if he'd watched what she did instead of what she'd said, he'd have been spared a lot of heartache.

The opening of the door broke into his reverie. Wanda stood there smiling. "Almost finished?" she asked cheerfully.

Emily said, "Almost. May we have a few more minutes?"

Wanda said, "Of course," and went back outside.

Emily looked at Cody and it wasn't at all the way Jessica had looked at him. Somehow he felt as if Emily really saw him.

She smiled. "It's hard, isn't it." Her voice was soft and intimate, so appealing that it took him a moment to respond.

"What's hard?"

"Answering all these personal questions." She wrinkled her pert little nose. "I mean, it's hard unless you sit around all day thinking deep thoughts about your life. Do you?"

He laughed, feeling some of his tension drain away. "Not too often. Guess you don't, either."

She made a rueful little face before turning back to the paper before her. Cody did likewise.

Ideal Partner Would Be, ''A good old down-home country girl without pretensions,'' he wrote. *What I'm Seeking In A Relationship*: love and marriage.

Last question. *Describe Yourself In Your Own Words*. He scowled at the paper for a long time, finally writing a single word: tall.

Emily had finished the questionnaire well before Cody but hadn't been satisfied with her answers. Going back over what she'd written, though, she couldn't find anything worth changing.

What difference did it make? It was all a pack of lies anyway. Still, she'd instinctively asked for more time when Wanda appeared. She didn't need it but had a sinking feeling that she wasn't going to like what came next.

Wanda reappeared a few minutes later, bustling over to the table with her eyes twinkling. ''There,'' she said, scooping up the questionnaires, ''that wasn't so hard, now was it?''

Cody groaned, which made Emily smile. She hadn't enjoyed it, either.

Wanda pursed her lips. ''Now, now, I know we ask a lot of nosy questions, but the computer needs to know!''

''I suppose.'' Cody rose, stretching his lanky frame. ''Now what?''

''Why, now we take a couple of pictures.''

''Pictures?'' Emily didn't much like the sound of that. She didn't like having her picture taken because she thought the result never looked like her.

"It's a very simple procedure," Wanda assured her. "The camera is all set up. I just plunk you down on the stool and say, 'Smile!'"

"And then what happens?" Cody asked again. "When will you have news for us?"

Wanda frowned thoughtfully. "Tomorrow," she announced, "unless George gets temperamental on me."

"Tomorrow!" Emily was astonished. "I wouldn't even think that would give you time to put our information in the computer, let alone get the results."

For the first time, Wanda looked flustered. "I'm very good with computers," she said defensively. "I know I didn't grow up with them the way you young people did, but—"

"Oh, Wanda, I didn't mean..." Emily hesitated, chewing on her lower lip. She wouldn't hurt this nice lady's feelings for the world. "I only meant that I didn't think *anybody* could work that fast. If you can, then I applaud you."

The old lady seemed to recover herself. "I guess I'm touchy about my age," she confided. "When George was installed, it took me *forever* to learn to get along with him. For a while there, I thought I might actually lose my job."

"Hey," Cody said, "you're not the only one with computer problems. Those blamed things can be more trouble than they're worth sometimes."

"You know, they really can." Wanda gave him a grateful glance. "Let's go get those pictures and then you can both run along. I'm sure you have many more important things to do today."

Cody grinned. "This is the most important thing

I've got to do, period. As far as I'm concerned, you can take all the time you need.''

He and Wanda turned expectantly to Emily. Cornered, she could only smile and agree. Even if it wasn't true. None of this had the least bit of importance to her. Except, of course, that she didn't want to hurt anyone's feelings.

Or get involved.

From: MataHari@Upzydazy.com
Sent: Monday, Nov. 2, 7:42 p.m.
To: SuperScribe@BoyHowdy.com
Subject: Hold your horses!
Calm down, will you, Terry? I said I'd go to the Yellow Rose and I did. Answered the usual nosy questions, had my picture taken, the whole nine yards. The lady I dealt with, Wanda Roland, is really nice. I also met a really cute guy. Almost makes me sorry this isn't for real. :-((Not really.) I'll let you know if and when I get matched, but in the meantime... Yellow Rose Matchmakers is located in a beautiful old Victorian house in a quiet and shady neighborhood...

CHAPTER TWO

From: SuperScribe@BoyHowdy.com
Sent: Tuesday, Nov. 3, 6:30 a.m.
To: MataHari@Upzydazy.com
Subject: Good girl!
I knew I could count on you, Emmy. Sorry if I pushed.
Here's a rose as a peace offering: @)->—>— Okay,
down to business. Wanda Roland is in my notes and I
want to know more about her, especially how she gets
on with the computers. There seems to be some ques-
tion about this "completely computerized" claim.
Also, be sure to keep me posted on your adventures
with the "really cute guy"....

EMILY downloaded her E-mail from her laptop computer first thing Tuesday morning and read Terry's
note at the breakfast table while Laurie looked on with
ill-concealed curiosity. When she'd finished the message, Emily wadded it into a ball, which she tossed
on the floor for her yellow cat, Archie, to bat around.

"I'm dying of curiosity!" Laurie announced.
"What did he say?"

"He who?" Emily reached for her glass of orange
juice, trying to compose herself. She wished to heaven
she'd never mentioned the "really cute guy".

"C'mon, that E-mail was from Terry, right? What
did that con man want this time?"

"That's no way to talk about my cousin," Emily

said primly, but she couldn't help smiling. She'd called him worse herself, but blood was still thicker than water.

"Don't forget, I know the guy," Laurie said darkly. "Old Anything-for-a-scoop Kirkwood."

"Give him a break. This is a new job and he's trying to make good." Emily uttered an exasperated sigh. "Do you realize you've made me defend him? I must be nuts."

"You sure are, after he basically blackmailed you into helping him research this story. He tried to pull the same stunt with me but he didn't have anything to hold over my head." Laurie took a sip of coffee. She was already dressed for work although she'd come in quite late the night before. This was the first chance the roommates had had to talk since breakfast yesterday.

"He didn't have to blackmail me," Emily said. "You know I owed him after he saved my father's life in that boating accident. I can never repay him for that."

"No, Em, your *father* can never repay him for that. Or couldn't—I guess now that he's dead, it kind of gets both of you off the hook."

"Really? Then why do I feel so beholden?"

Laurie shrugged. "Because you're one of the good guys," she said with a smile. "You'd probably help Terry even if he wasn't your cousin and you didn't think you owed him." She grinned and added, "But it's still blackmail!"

"You could be right."

Laurie returned to the main point. "Was Terry happy you've been to the Yellow Rose?"

Emily nodded. "My...counselor or whatever you call her is a delightful old lady named Wanda Roland. I mentioned her in my E-mail to Terry yesterday and he's apparently heard of her. He wants to know all about her and how she gets along with computers."

"That sounds innocent enough."

"Yes, except...there's something funny about Wanda and computers."

"Funny ha-ha or funny strange?"

"Definitely funny strange. She talks about using them, even boasts about how computerized the company is, but she touches her computer the way I'd touch a snake."

"Not with love, huh."

"Definitely not." Emily frowned. "She calls her computer George."

"That *is* peculiar. Most computers I know are named Max." Laurie laughed. "So did anything else happen yesterday, except that you met a strange little old lady?"

"Well..." Don't go on, Emily warned herself. Don't mention Cody James. She'd never see him again, so why bring him up? "I...uh..." She licked her lips, surprised at the unexpected desire to talk about him. "I met a really good-looking man. I mean, *really*."

"Better-looking than John?"

"Much better-looking."

Laurie rubbed her hands together with glee. "Now we're getting down to brass tacks!"

"But I don't *want* to get down to brass tacks. After John, I'm not in the market for a man, as you well know."

For a moment, Laurie frowned at her friend. Then she shook her head sadly. "Emily Kirkwood, I don't understand you at all. Just because your former fiancé was a louse doesn't mean they all are. Every woman without a man is in the market for one, preferably the right one, of course."

"That's just it. You never know if he's the right one until it's too late. And he doesn't know if *you're* the right one, either."

Laurie winked broadly. "Half the fun's in finding out."

"No, thank you very much. I'm only doing this to help my cousin research a magazine article so he can make good at his job. I'm definitely not looking for a relationship."

"You're sure about that?"

Emily lifted her chin. "Absolutely sure."

But if she *was* looking for a relationship—she pulled such thoughts up short. She had to forget Cody James and go to work! With any luck, today would *not* be the day she heard from Wanda Roland. In fact, if Emily was really lucky, Wanda wouldn't find a match anywhere inside that darned computer.

Cody was surprised to find his niece, ten-year-old Liana, at the lunch table when he came in from running longhorns on the north forty. "What you doin' home from school, shrimp?" he inquired, ruffling her straight dark hair.

Her mother, Elena, scowled from her spot before the built-in cooktop. Most family meals at the Flying J were taken in the large kitchen with everyone clustered around the big round oak table. The ranch hands ate at the chuck wagon, their own "café" staffed with a cook who made her way to the ranch each day from a nearby farm. Cody and his brother, Ben, Elena's husband, were as likely to eat the midday meal at one place as the other.

"Liana woke up this morning claiming to be sick," Elena said. "Silly me, I believed her."

Liana's lower lip thrust out in a pout. "I am sick," she whined. "I mean, I was, only now I feel better. Can I go out with Uncle Cody this afternoon, Mama? Can I?"

"No way." Elena used a spatula to dish up grilled steak-and-cheese sandwiches to augment the tomato soup already steaming in mugs. "If you're sick enough to stay home from school, you're too sick to get out of bed."

"I'm out of bed now," Liana argued, snatching a golden triangle off the platter when her mother set it down.

"Meals don't count. As soon as you finish…" Elena pointed toward the door leading to the stairs, which in turn led to the bedrooms.

"Uncle Cody!"

"Sorry, cupcake, your mother's right." He settled into his seat and warmed his hands around the mug of soup. It was chillier than usual out there today.

Elena smiled, her beautiful white teeth flashing. Ben had found a real jewel in her. "That's what I like about you, Cody," she said. "You never let them get the best of you."

Cody winked at Liana. "Never?"

Elena laughed. "Not that I know of anyway. So tell me, how did it go yesterday at the Yellow Rose?"

"All right," he said in a noncommittal tone. Although his entire family knew all about his decision to go wife-hunting, he felt uncharacteristically shy about yesterday.

Elena's brows rose. "You mean…?"

Just then, Ben entered through the back door, yanking off his denim jacket and tossing it onto a hook beside the door. "I'm hungry enough to eat a horse," the manager and co-owner of the Flying J declared. He paused long enough to drop a kiss on his wife's cheek on his way to wash up.

Watching them together, smiling and happy after twelve years of marriage, Cody felt envy start to boil in his chest. He fought it down valiantly. *That* was why he'd taken his courage in hand and gone to Yellow Rose Matchmakers; he wanted what Ben and Elena had. That included little Liana, grinning after her tall father with adoration in her eyes, and eight-year-old Jimmy, who was at school.

Elena smiled at her husband's broad back. "I was asking your brother how it went at the matchmaker's yesterday."

Ben grinned over his shoulder, busily splashing his hands beneath the stream of water. "Yeah, Cody, tell us all about it."

"Had to fill out a lot of junk," Cody said. He made a face.

"Like what?" Elena pressed.

"Ah, you know—what kinda guy I am, what kinda woman I'm looking for, stuff like that."

"Aunt Jessica was pretty," Liana piped up.

"Yeah," Cody agreed, "but I'm not lookin' for another one of those. Although…"

Elena and Ben both perked up. Ben dried his hands on a dish towel and joined them at the table. "Although what?"

"Well...I met a real looker while I was there."

Husband and wife exchanged knowing glances. "You did?" Elena asked encouragingly.

"But I'll never see that one again. It was just a screwup over the appointments." Cody helped himself to several sandwich halves from the platter, then reached for the jar of pickles.

"How can you be so sure?" Elena leaned forward on her elbows, apparently more interested in her brother-in-law's love life than in lunch.

"For openers, she's too good-looking."

"Uncle Cody doesn't trust pretty women," Liana announced with youthful authority.

All three adults stared at her, dumbfounded.

Flustered, she tried to regroup. "Well, I heard him say that to Daddy one time," she wailed.

Elena shook her head. "Little pitchers have big ears," she announced.

Ben laughed. "Little pitchers have got the straight of it this time. Okay, little brother, she's too good-looking. What else is wrong with her?"

"She's not interested in marriage."

"How can you be so sure of that?" Elena demanded.

"She said so."

The minute he made that announcement, he realized his mistake. Jessica had consistently said one thing and meant another. Maybe this woman meant one thing and *said* another. In which case, Cody's interest might not be as misplaced as he'd—

The telephone on the wall near the door began to ring and Elena went to answer it. After the briefest of conversations, she turned back with a big smile on her face. "That was a lady from Yellow Rose Matchmakers, Wanda something—"

"Wanda Roland." Cody's stomach clenched in the kind of anticipation he hadn't expected to feel. "What did she say?"

"That she's made a match for you. She wants you to come to her office this afternoon at four to hear the good news."

"Good news? How does she know it'll be good news? It could be a disaster. It could be—"

"Look, Daddy," Liana said, grinning. "Uncle Cody's scared!"

He sure was. Scared to death.

Emily was having a tough day at work. As temporary office manager for a brand-new branch of A&B Construction, she had more than enough to keep her busy. When her boss, Don Phillips, poked his head in, she had a whole list of questions for him.

Don was big and bluff and hearty, not to mention a great boss. In his mid-forties, he treated everyone who worked for A&B the same, although he was a partner in the business he'd helped build from the ground up. When all her questions had been answered and decisions made, he refilled his coffee cup and lingered.

"So how are you liking San Antonio?" he asked. "Had a chance to look around?"

"Not much. It's pretty, though. I saw that right away."

Don nodded. "That it is. I'm sorry I've been such a slave driver."

"You haven't! Just yesterday, I took an extra long lunch." To go to a dating agency, but he didn't need to know that.

He chuckled. "But you worked the entire weekend. Don't think I wasn't aware of it. And you work late almost every night. You'll probably only be in San Antonio for a few months, so you need to get out and see—"

The telephone on her desk started ringing. With a nod of apology, she picked it up. "A&B Construction."

"Is that you, Emily dear?"

"Wanda?" Surely she hadn't made a match already! Emily's heart fluttered.

"How flattering. You remember my voice. I've called to tell you that George has found a match for you already. Isn't that good news?"

"Wonderful."

"Yes, well, I wonder if you could come to the office at four o'clock?"

"Four o'clock today?" Emily's mind raced, coming up with all kinds of reasons why it was impossible. "I'm afraid that's completely out of the question. I—"

Don interrupted her. "Whatever it is, go ahead. Wasn't I just telling you not to work so hard?"

Emily felt a touch of panic. "But—"

"Hey, who's the boss here?" He rose, placed his coffee cup on the desk and picked up his hard hat. "Just lock up when you go and put the Back Tomorrow sign on the door."

"Oh, Don, I really don't want to cause anyone any inconvenience."

"Not a problem. Just do it."

Emily sat there with one hand over the mouthpiece. There was simply no way to get out of this. Taking a deep breath, she removed her hand and said, "All right, Wanda. I'll be there at four."

"That's wonderful! See you then." Wanda's relief came through loud and clear.

Emily hung up, wondering at her reluctance to see this charade through to a speedy end so she could be free of her obligation. And then she remembered Cody James and realized that no matter whom George had matched her with, he was bound to be a big letdown.

Cody walked into Yellow Rose Matchmakers at 4:03 and found Emily standing in front of the receptionist with a puzzled expression on her beautiful face. He couldn't help smiling at the pretty picture she made in her pink suit with her blond hair tousled around her face by the wind.

She saw him and did a double take. "What are *you* doing here?" she demanded.

Slightly taken aback by her lack of enthusiasm, he shrugged. "Wanda called. I have a four o'clock appointment."

"Oh, dear." Teresa grimaced. "Don't tell me she's done it again."

Emily sighed. "Looks like." To Cody, she added, "I apologize if I sounded unfriendly a minute ago. I was just surprised to see you again, that's all."

"Me, too." But for him, the surprise had been

pleasant. To Teresa, he said, "Does this happen often?"

"Often? No." She rolled her eyes. "Occasionally...yes. But Wanda has such a great instinct for matchmaking that we tend to overlook it." She frowned. "You two aren't upset, are you? I suppose I could always assign one or the other of you to a different mentor—that's what we call them, mentors—maybe Miss Willie or Moira can help?"

"No!" they exclaimed in unison, then exchanged surprised glances.

Emily added, "I wouldn't want to cause Wanda any trouble. It could happen to anyone."

"Yeah," Cody agreed. "Besides, I'll be glad to let the lady go first."

"Thank you," Emily said firmly, "but that's not necessary. We could...we could draw straws or something. Just because you're a man is no reason for you to go last."

"It's reason enough for me," Cody said. "My daddy didn't bring me up to—"

"Hold on, both of you." When Teresa had the floor, she continued, "Wanda called just a few minutes ago to say she's running late. She'll be here in—" she checked her watch "—about thirty-five minutes. She hopes you can both wait."

"Oh, dear." Emily looked positively exasperated.

"No problem," Cody said, hoping to set a good example for patience and understanding. "Should we just wait here?" He glanced around the reception area.

"Sure, or maybe..." Teresa looked thoughtful. "There's a coffee shop just a couple of blocks away.

Maybe you'd like to kill a few minutes there and then come back about five?''

Cody looked at Emily and Emily looked at Cody, and something seemed to click; her expression softened and he knew what her answer would be before she said it.

''If it's all right with you, Cody...?''

''I'll drive,'' he said. ''See you at five, Teresa.''

Holding the door for Emily to precede him, Cody realized he didn't mind waiting at all...with her.

''Wanna piece of pie with that coffee? It's homemade.''

Cody looked at Emily, who smiled and shook her head. But she wasn't surprised when he hesitated.

''What kind?''

''We got apple, cherry, lemon and...'' The waitress craned her head to view the pie case behind the counter. ''Looks like pumpkin, but I won't guarantee it.''

''I'll take a slab of apple. Could you warm that up and throw a scoop of vanilla ice cream at it?''

The waitress grinned. Cody sure knew how to warm up strangers. ''Glad to do it, cowboy.'' She headed for that pie case.

Emily stirred a packet of sweetener into her coffee, feeling strangely ill at ease. They hadn't talked at all on the short ride over in the battered old red pickup truck with the big *J* painted on the side—with wings yet. Now the silence would have to be broken.

Cody took a gulp of hot black coffee. ''Isn't this better than sittin' in a waiting room?'' he asked rhetorically.

"Much better," she agreed, although she wasn't quite sure about that. "Do you have far to drive to get here?"

"Seventy-five miles or thereabouts, depending on which part of the ranch I start from."

She was impressed. "That's quite a drive."

He shrugged. "I'm used to it."

The waitress put a huge piece of steaming pie in front of him, ice cream already beginning to melt in a creamy puddle around it. He gave her a quick smile of thanks and picked up his fork.

"How about you?" he asked, the first bite hovering above the plate. "Where do you live?"

"Not far from here. I share an apartment in a converted Victorian with a friend."

He chewed thoughtfully before answering. "Not a male friend, I take it. Otherwise you wouldn't be here."

"That's a safe bet." She looked away from those probing blue eyes at several people perched on stools at the counter.

"Why *are* you here?"

Rattled, she jerked back around. "You mean here at this café or there at the Yellow Rose?"

"Let's start with the Rose."

She licked her lips, fumbling for an answer. "All the usual reasons," she hedged, "exactly as I said before. I'm new in town, I don't know many people—"

"Any woman who looks like you doesn't need to go to a dating agency to meet people, at least not to meet *men* people."

That was exactly what she thought about him and *women* people. "If that's a compliment, thank you."

"It's a compliment."

"What about you? Why are you here?"

"Here at the café or there at the Rose?" He gave her that crooked little grin that was so charming. "I'm here because I was curious about you and wanted to know more. I'm *there* because I want to get married and have a passel of kids."

"That makes sense," she said, "I guess."

He finished the pie, placed the fork on the plate and slid it aside. "But you said you're not interested in marriage."

She lifted her chin. "That's right."

"Why not?"

"Because there'll be plenty of time for that later."

"Are you one of those career women, then?"

"Not exactly. I mean, I have a job I like but I don't see it as a *career*, exactly."

"Ahh," he said wisely, "I see."

His tone annoyed her. "*What* do you see?"

"You've been burned. Some guy done you wrong and you're having a hard time getting over it."

"Why, of all the—that's not it at all!" But it was. She'd been burned not once but twice, and *two* men had indeed done her wrong: the man who'd dumped her, and the man with whom her mother had run away when Emily was twelve. Both were rich and handsome and thought they could buy anything they wanted.

Unfortunately, in the case of Beverly Kirkwood, that had proven to be true. But when her lover tried to use his enormous wealth and power to gain custody of Emily, the child had dug in her heels and fought to stay with the father who had not betrayed her. The legal battles had gone on for years and left her father broken in spirit as well as financially.

"I'm sorry," Cody said, and he did look contrite. "I didn't mean to upset you. It just seemed so obvious."

"Not as obvious as you might think," she said grimly. "I suppose eventually I'll want what most women want—a husband, children—but for now I'm just looking for a good time." Better than saying all she was looking for was to discharge a moral obligation to her cousin so she could settle back down to her usual quiet existence.

That lopsided grin made her stomach do flip-flops. "Damn shame," Cody drawled, "but I kinda know where you're coming from. You see, I had a wife who could stop traffic, she was so good-lookin'. When the marriage didn't work out, I got soured on pretty women." He looked down at his coffee cup, then slanted her a quick glance. "Like you, for instance."

"Me?" She'd never thought of herself as anything special in the looks department. All right…passable, certainly…but a traffic stopper?

He laughed. "Don't look so surprised. The truth is, we're as different as night and day."

She grinned back, relieved that he'd realized that. "You say pa-tay-toe, I say pa-tah-toe."

"Exactly. I like horses and cows and you…"

"Like ballet and concerts. I like cats and you like…"

"Dogs. I like the country…"

"And I like the city."

"Tough break." With those words, all his good humor went right out the window.

"There's plenty of fish in the sea," she said lightly, not sure whether she believed that or not.

"I'm not looking for a fish."

"Neither am I."

Their glances locked and tension sizzled between them. After a very long moment, he said, "I hate not knowing."

"N-not knowing what?"

"What might have been. We'll go back to Wanda's office and she'll flutter around and give you some fancy guy who likes fancy stuff, and she'll give me some country girl who likes country stuff, and we'll both be better off. But I'll probably always wonder what might have been."

"But we have to go along with whatever Wanda says," she reminded him. "I mean, she's the expert, right?" Her stomach hurt when she said it.

"Right." His face, in repose, looked strong and a little sad.

"I mean, she has George to help her out. We can't fight modern science and all that."

"Absolutely not."

"Well, then." Feeling jumpy and out of sync, she glanced at her watch. "Hey, it's time to get back."

"If you say so." He hauled a wallet from his back pocket. He pulled out a bill and dropped it on the table. His gaze captured hers again. "I still say it's a shame, even if it is for the best."

"It's definitely for the best. Whatever Wanda says will have to be the way it is." But in her heart, she felt a sadness she couldn't explain.

*   *   *

During the short ride back to the Yellow Rose, Cody thought about all they'd said. Even though they'd probably never see each other again after today, he was glad she didn't know the truth about him: that his family was one of the most successful ranching dynasties in Texas. He wouldn't want her if she was just after his money; been there, done that. He'd rather have her think of him, if she ever did, as a simple cowboy.

No harm done.

Back at the Rose, he followed her up the steps and into the pretty yellow Victorian. Teresa looked up with alarm on her face.

"Oh, dear, I don't even want to face you two."

Emily stiffened. "What now?"

"Wanda won't be able to make it at all, I'm afraid. She wonders if you could come back Friday morning at nine."

"What?" Emily looked distraught, a pretty strong reaction for a woman who claimed she wasn't all that interested in a relationship anyway.

Not that Cody was all that interested in driving all the way back into San Antonio again so soon, either. "Maybe we should forget the whole thing," he suggested.

"That's what I'm thinking," Emily agreed.

"Please don't," Teresa pleaded. "You see, Wanda was in a minor traffic accident on her way here."

Emily gasped. "Oh, my gosh! Is she all right?"

"Yes, but she's pretty shaken. She feels terrible about this, but—"

"No problem," Cody said quickly. "We didn't understand. We don't *really* mind coming back, right, Emily?"

He saw the struggle on her face, but then she nodded. "You're right. Friday at nine will be just fine."

Should he ask her out to dinner since they were here with nothing to do? Should he suggest they meet for breakfast before their appointment? Should he—

"Thanks for the coffee, Cody." She gave him a brief, impersonal nod. "Perhaps I'll see you tomorrow."

Watching her let herself out the heavy front door, he knew for sure what he should have done.

He should have acted faster.

From: MataHari@Upzydazy.com
Sent: Tuesday, Nov. 3, 7:13 p.m.
To: SuperScribe@BoyHowdy.com
Subject: Bummer day!
Today, cousin dear, was a waste of time. I didn't even *see* Wanda Roland so there's nothing new on that front. I have yet another appointment Friday morning and maybe I'll have more to tell you after that. In the meantime, suffice it to say that I am *not* having a good time....

CHAPTER THREE

From: SuperScribe@BoyHowdy.com
Sent: Thursday, Nov. 5, 7:11 p.m.
To: MataHari@Upzydazy.com
Subject: Just curious.
So you won't see Wanda Roland until tomorrow, huh.
That *is* a bummer, but at least you're trying. I do
like what you've given me so far. You didn't mention
the "really cute guy" again. Guess that means he was
a no-show, too....

KEEP believing that, Terry, Emily thought as she reread yesterday's E-mail missive from her cousin.
Sitting in the reception area at Yellow Rose
Matchmakers, she assured herself that there was no
reason her entire life had to be an open book.

She'd arrived a few minutes early for her appointment and now, on the stroke of nine, the front door
swung open and Cody James entered. Feeling guilty
for no particular reason, she stuffed Terry's E-mail
into her jacket pocket and gave Cody a deliberately
impersonal smile.

Before he could even speak to Teresa, Wanda's
door popped open. "How lovely! You're both here.
Please come in, children."

Cody looked at Emily and Emily looked at Cody.
It was as if Wanda's announcement ended even this
tenuous relationship between them. Once matched

with different people, they'd go their separate ways and that would be that.

"After you," he said.

She nodded her thanks and preceded him into the office, feeling intensely his presence just behind her. She'd never met a more magnetic man. When he was in the room, it was as if her entire being was somehow connected to his every move.

Silly. He certainly wasn't her type. Too good-looking, for openers. Too different in his dreams, for closers.

"Sit down, children, do sit down." Wanda indicated the same seats they'd occupied before. Turning, she limped behind the desk.

Emily exchanged an alarmed glance with Cody, who looked equally concerned. "Are you all right?" Emily asked the little woman. "Teresa said your accident wasn't serious."

Wanda waved concern aside. "No, no, I'm fine. A little stiff is all. That's to be expected at my age."

Emily felt greatly relieved. "Thank heaven. Uhh...you have something to tell us?"

"That's right."

Wanda just sat there, smiling. Watching attentively, Emily thought she saw a bruise on the woman's forehead. Perhaps she'd been hurt more seriously than she'd admitted.

Finally, Cody cleared his throat. "We're both a little curious how you happened to double up on our appointments again," he said. A glance at Emily drew a nod of agreement. "Not that we mind."

Another nod from Emily, this one less enthusiastic. Actually, she did mind. She felt uncomfortable around

Cody, mostly because she was so attracted to him and knew such feelings were a complete waste of time.

"My goodness, why should you mind?" Wanda cocked her head and furrowed her brow. "I thought you'd have guessed by now."

"Guessed what?" they asked together. This time, Emily and Cody exchanged frowns.

"Why, guessed that the two of you are made for each other. In fact, this is a match made in heaven!"

Emily gasped and fell back in her chair. "You've got to be kidding!"

Wanda looked hurt. "George never kids," she said with great dignity, "and he never lies."

"Is George ever wrong?" Cody sounded grim.

Wanda blinked her big blue eyes. "Not to my knowledge," she said, frowning. "I thought you'd both be thrilled. It was obvious to me from the beginning that you belong together forever."

"But, Wanda," Emily protested, "we're so different!"

"Opposites attract," Wanda said serenely.

"We came here for different reasons," Cody argued.

"That's what makes a horse race."

Cody looked around, a desperate gleam in his eyes. "But Emily isn't interested in marriage and I won't settle for anything less."

"It's a woman's prerogative to change her mind."

"But I don't *want* to change my mind!"

"A woman can even change her mind about changing her mind," Wanda pointed out. She pursed her soft lips. "I don't know what's the matter with you two," she grumbled. "Did you come here because you want the help of a professional or not?"

"Well, yes," Cody admitted.

"And a computer," Emily chimed in. "I wanted the latest and most up-to-date guidance to be had."

Wanda threw up her hands. "That's what you're getting, so what's the problem?"

"Well..." Emily thought fast. "Could I see the computer printout for this match? I'd like to know just what George found about the two of us that's so compatible."

Wanda gasped. "No one has ever asked for such a thing."

Even Cody looked puzzled by that. "Never?"

Wanda shook her silvery head.

"I'd really like to see that printout." Emily felt she must stand firm. Here was a chance to get the information Terry needed, which would get him off her back once and for all.

Wanda grimaced and drummed her fingers on the desktop. With extreme reluctance, she said, "Of course, if you insist, I suppose I can try."

"Try?" Emily echoed.

"George is *so* temperamental. Sometimes he gets his feelings hurt and then you don't know what he..." As she spoke, she reached out with one hesitant forefinger to touch the keyboard. Instantly, she jerked back with a gasp.

Cody half rose from his chair. "What is it? Did George—did you get shocked or something?"

"The screen went blank!"

"The screen went...?" Cody walked around the desk until he could see the front of the computer. He frowned, leaned down and hit a couple of keys, then shook his head. "She's right," he said to Emily. "Nothing."

"Is it broken?" Something fishy was going on here, Emily just couldn't imagine what.

Wanda shook her head furiously. "Not broken. This happens now and again. George is temperamental, just like I told you. Give him a little time and he'll be all right."

Emily grimaced. "I'm not sure I want a temperamental computer deciding my future."

"Wait just a cotton-pickin' minute." Cody looked annoyed in the extreme. "I think we already discussed this, Emily. I'm as convinced as you are that as a pair, we're a bust."

"And your point is…?"

"You're talkin' about me as if I were Jack the Ripper or something. I don't think it would hurt either of us to give George and Wanda the benefit of the doubt here."

"Meaning…?"

"Meaning I'm perfectly willing to spend a little time with you—just until Wanda gets George up and running and rechecks the data, that is."

Emily stared at him. "You know I'm not your type."

"That's true."

"But you're still willing to waste your time—"

"See, there you go with that negative talk again. I'm sayin', let's be fair about this. They—I mean *she* is the professional. If Wanda says we're compatible, we must *be* compatible on some level."

"More than compatible," Wanda put in, "much more. As I said, a match made in heaven."

"More like a *mis*match made in heaven," Emily muttered.

"What's that?" Cody asked quickly.

"Nothing. I was thinking aloud."

All at once everyone quit talking. Emily chewed on her lower lip, trying to figure a way out of this without hurting anyone's feelings. Differences aside, she found Cody way too appealing to risk spending time with him when it couldn't possibly lead anywhere. How was she going to get out of this?

Puzzling over her options, she suddenly became aware of the fragrance of roses permeating the air. She looked up and her gaze caught on his and held until she felt dizzy from staring into his beautiful blue eyes. He made things even tougher when he smiled that crooked little smile that took her breath away.

"I'm willing to take a chance if you are," he said.

No formed on the tip of Emily's tongue. She didn't dare spend time with him. But before she could refuse, Wanda clapped her hands together as if with great glee.

"Of course she will," Wanda cried.

Cody leaned forward with his hands on the desktop, his voice firm. "And in the meantime, Wanda, you have to promise you'll recheck the data with George, like Emily wants."

"Absolutely." She was the picture of trustworthiness and good cheer.

Then why, Emily wondered, don't I trust her? And equally important, why don't I trust George? It's as if she *told* him to roll over and play dead!

*　　*　　*

Emily and Cody stood on the front porch of the Yellow Rose. She looked so uncomfortable that he almost felt sorry for her. Reluctantly, he concluded that he must give her a way out. "If you really think this is such a horrible idea—"

"No, no, that's not it. Exactly." She stuffed her hands into the pockets of her suede jacket.

A breeze ruffled her blond hair and he longed to reach out and smooth it back into place. "What, then? We're not talking about a lasting commitment or anything at this point, just a date or two while Wanda gets her act together."

Emily grimaced, her lips finally curving into a reluctant smile. "You think that'll happen in only a date or two?"

He smiled back. "Maybe...if they're long dates. *Really* long dates." Hell, he wouldn't care how long they were if they gave him time to figure her out.

"I think you're being a bit optimistic." She edged closer to the top step, glancing at her watch. "I really have to get back to work now."

"Me, too. Uhh...how about tonight?"

She blinked. "What about tonight?"

"Wanna go out?"

"You mean, on a *date*?"

She looked so flustered that he had to laugh. "That's what this is all about, remember?"

Her expression was rueful. "I remember, but tonight's not good. I'm going to have to work late to make up for all the time I've spent at the Yellow Rose lately."

Oh, oh, he thought, the bum's rush. Not one to

concede defeat, he pressed on, "How about tomorrow night, then?" He waited for her to turn him down.

She drew in a deep breath and said, "Okay."

He blinked. "Really? You'll go out with me?"

She nodded. "I live at 7888 Carter Street. It's—"

"I'll find it."

She nodded. "Seven o'clock?"

"Fine."

"Uhh…what are we doing?"

"What do you want to do?"

"What do *you* want to do?"

"When a beautiful woman asks a man what he wants to do—"

"Forget I said anything." Color brightened her high cheekbones. She started down the steps, a copy of Cody's original questionnaire in her hand. "Maybe we can just have a drink and get to know each other a little better. Nothing formal or anything."

"Sounds like a winner," he called after her, thinking of honky-tonk bars and slow dancing in the shadows.

That, of course, was before he got back to the ranch and read her questionnaire.

By the time seven o'clock rolled around Saturday night, Emily was a nervous wreck. Even the cats seemed to sense it, slinking away every time she entered a room. When the bell rang, she jumped a foot and stood there staring at the door as if it posed some kind of threat.

Laurie, seated at one end of the couch where she could keep an interested eye on the proceedings, grinned. "That door won't answer itself," she declared. "C'mon, Emmy, I'm dying to meet this guy."

Now there's a thought, Emily told herself. Laurie's much more his type than I am and she'd just broken up with her boyfriend last week. Maybe, just maybe...

Emily threw open the door and there he stood, more than six feet of gorgeous guy in jeans and boots, a red Western-cut shirt and shiny leather jacket. He held his hat in one hand and a single yellow rose in the other. His blue gaze traveled over her with approval.

Emily took a quick step back, gesturing him to enter. She hadn't known how to dress for this evening and had settled on black silk pants and a white silk shirt. From the look on his face, he approved her choice.

"Cody," she said in a voice more breathless than it should have been, "this is my roommate, Laurie Billingsley. Laurie, this is—"

"Oh, my, I *know* who this is." Beaming, Laurie leaped from the couch and darted forward, her hand outstretched. She shot Emily a quick glance. "Your description was *perfect*."

Cody looked confused. "Nice to meet you, Laurie." He thrust the rose at Emily and his other hand closed over Laurie's. All of a sudden, he yelped and jumped back, releasing her hand as if she'd shocked him.

He looked down and so did everyone else. What they saw was Emily's calico cat, Chloe, twining around his legs.

Emily snatched up the cat. "Sorry about that," she said. "I know you don't like cats."

He looked at the cat with distaste. "It just surprised me."

"I read your questionnaire," she reminded him, hugging the cat as if she expected Cody to do it harm. "You said cats were your least favorite animal."

"At the time I wrote that, I didn't know any cats personally." Reaching out, he curved his forefinger to scratch Chloe behind one ear. She purred and arched toward him, almost wiggling out of Emily's arms. "We've got cats at the ranch," he went on, "but they live in the barns and chase rats and mice. They're a pretty wild bunch."

"I have a cat," Laurie put in. "He's around here somewhere."

Emily smiled at Cody, smiling at Chloe. "Do you really have a pet buffalo?"

"Buffalo!" Laurie echoed. "You've got a pet…?"

He grinned. "Doesn't everyone? I'll have to introduce you to Nickel one of these days."

"Nickel?" Laurie repeated, quickly adding, "Oh, I get it, the buffalo on the coin."

"That's right." Cody gave her an absent glance. "Are you ready to go, Emily?"

She was as ready as she'd ever be. She nodded, aware of the delicate aroma of the rose she still held.

"Nice meeting you, Laurie. You, too, Chloe."

Laurie muttered thanks. Chloe leaped from Emily's arms and dashed behind the couch. Emily took a deep breath, grabbed up her jacket and marched out the door, still holding her rose.

Cody had had a helluva time trying to figure out where to take her.

If she had read his questionnaire, he had *pored* over hers. He'd discovered that they were every bit as different as they'd thought. Jeez, she was a vegetarian, the worst blow of all to a cattle rancher. For the first time, he'd questioned his own sanity for pursuing her.

She also liked pop music while he went in for country and western. Where did that leave him in his effort to come up with a suitable compromise for their first date?

He finally concluded that it left him with the Menger Bar. It might be part of a classy historic hotel of the same name, but more cattle deals had probably been made in the Menger since it opened in 1859 than any other single spot in Texas. With that destination in mind, he pointed his pickup truck toward Alamo Plaza and Crockett Street.

She didn't ask questions and he was forced to conclude that she either trusted him to pick an appropriate place or was waiting for him to fall on his face. Conversation was light and sporadic until he turned onto Crockett, at which time she gasped and pointed to the old Spanish mission across from the hotel.

"My gosh, is that the Alamo?"

He had to chuckle at the awe in her voice. "I take it you haven't had time yet to do the tourist thing."

"No, but I'm dying to. Every Texan wants to see the Alamo!"

"Now you have. Maybe next time we go out, we can go inside."

"Next time?" She slanted him a dubious glance.

"If there is a next time," he agreed calmly. "Now if I can just find a place to park..."

He lucked out on that one, finding a spot only a

block from the hotel. Now all he had to worry about was the rest of the evening....

Emily looked around the Menger Bar with complete approval. "This place is wonderful," she said to Cody, sitting across from her at the small wooden table. The bar was packed, but almost as if it were ordained, this table had been vacated just as they walked inside.

He smiled. "I've always liked it."

She looked with approval at the darkly gleaming bar, at the beveled mirrors and paneled ceiling. The quiet opulence spoke of an understated elegance long past. "Is this bar as old as it looks?" she ventured.

"Late 1880s, if I've got my dates right. It's a replica of the House of Lords Pub in London, as exact as they could get it."

"I'm impressed."

The waiter brought their drinks: beer for him, white wine for her. He lifted his drink. "Cheers."

"Cheers."

They drank.

He picked up the conversation. "A lot of famous people have come through here. This is where Teddy Roosevelt recruited his Rough Riders for the Spanish-American War, and Carry Nation and her Women's Temperance Union took an ax to that very bar."

"That's wonderful! Who else dropped by the Menger?"

"General Robert E. Lee rode his horse into the hotel lobby, but that was before this bar was built. They also say there are ghosts here...."

They talked on about pleasant, impersonal things.

Emily felt herself relaxing, warming toward him. One drink stretched to two; he ordered nachos and they munched on tortilla chips and melted cheese and talked about the Menger and the Alamo and San Antonio itself.

"I think I'm going to like it here," Emily admitted, "although I wasn't exactly pleased when my company asked me to accept a temporary transfer."

He frowned. "Temporary?"

She nodded. "Once the new office is up and running, I'll be heading back to Dallas."

"When will that be?"

"Sometime in February most likely."

"I see." He turned his drink around in his hands. "That doesn't give us—give me much time."

"Time for what?" she asked suspiciously.

His smile was warm and intimate. "Time to get to know you. Guess I'll have to speed up the timetable." He leaned across the small table and planted a quick kiss on her lips. Before she could protest, he stood and offered her his hand.

She took it without thinking and he drew her to her feet. She was still tingling from the quick, unexpected brush of his lips.

"We're going?" she inquired breathlessly.

He nodded. "When you read my questionnaire, did you get past the part about cats?"

"Yes."

"Then you saw that my tastes in food and music aren't the same as yours." He led her toward the door. Once on the sidewalk, he turned to her. "Now we're going to one of my favorite places. Just to see if you can take it, you know?"

She nodded. "Fair is fair," she agreed. "I don't know how you guessed I'd like the Menger since it's neither vegetarian nor pop, but you were right."

"Now I'm guessing you'll like Josie's," he said. "Let's go."

She did like Josie's, despite the fact that she'd spent very little time in honky-tonk bars full of rowdy cowboys and country music. The friendly waitress called Cody "hon" and directed them to an empty booth so close to the stage that there was nothing to do but dance since they'd have to scream to be heard above the band.

Dancing with Cody didn't turn out to be a chore even though the Texas two-step was not exactly Emily's long suit. At first she stepped on his feet so regularly that she tried to coax him off the floor, but he laughed and pulled her back into his arms. Soon they were threading their way through the throng on the crowded floor as if they'd been dancing together all their lives.

Emily was taken aback by the pleasure to be found pressed against his tall body, shielded by his strong arms. She'd never felt so safe in her life—or so endangered. He was just too darn sexy for her peace of mind. The light but insistent pressure of his hand on the small of her back brought her closer still, until they truly moved as one.

The music ended. When he would have moved them smoothly into the next number, she shook her head, pointing toward their booth.

"I think it's time to go," she shouted to be heard

above the din. She glanced at her watch but couldn't make out the time in the dim light.

He hesitated, then smiled and mouthed the words, "Whatever you say."

Had he agreed so readily because he was a nice guy or because he wasn't as caught up in the moment as she had been? She worried about that all the way back to her apartment, where he pulled to the curb and turned off the engine. By the illumination of a streetlight, he turned toward her on the bench seat. Touching her chin gently, he tilted up her face.

"So what's the verdict?" he asked.

She could see the outline of his face but not his expression, although she supposed he could see her well enough. Well enough that she didn't think she could get away with lying to him. "I had a nice time, if that's what you're asking."

"That's the first part of what I'm asking." He shifted his fingers until he cupped her chin. "What are you going to tell Wanda when she calls you tomorrow?"

"She doesn't even know we've gone out. What makes you think she's going to call me tomorrow?"

"She's going to want to know if we hit it off. I want to know that, too."

"Cody, I..." Emily drew in a deep breath. "This is no good. We both know it."

"*Did* we hit it off?"

"We're too different. Wanda is utterly wrong about us."

"Utterly?"

Was he moving closer? Was his head beginning a slow descent...?

"I had a lovely evening," she said quickly. "You're a wonderful guide. I truly appreciate your patience." Why was she suddenly speaking in short, staccato sentences?

"I had a lovely evening, too. Lovely enough that I'd like to do it again. Just while we wait for Wanda to correct her mistake, of course."

Emily groaned. "But, Cody, that might take a little time."

"I've got time. Will you go out with me again, Emily?"

"I—w-when? I'm really busy...."

"Tomorrow."

"I couldn't possibly."

"Monday? Tuesday? Name it."

All her resolve was crumbling around her. She chewed on her lower lip, sensed he was watching her do it and stopped. "Friday night?"

"A week, huh. Okay, Friday works."

He turned and threw open his door. Emily sat there breathing hard, feeling as if she'd just dodged a bullet. She'd been so sure he was going to kiss her. She was so grateful he hadn't.

She was so *disappointed* he hadn't.

He opened her door and reached for her, his hands closing around her waist. Instead of merely helping her out of the pickup, he lifted her, then lowered her slowly, her body sliding against his.

When she stood before him, staring up in shocked reaction, he grinned. "That wasn't so hard," he said in a teasing tone. Before she could respond, he covered her lips with his.

Emily felt as if she'd stuck her finger in a light

socket. His kiss transported her instantly to a state of bliss she'd never before experienced. Without conscious decision, she curved her arms around his neck and kissed him back.

She had only one thought in her befuddled brain. *And I thought we had nothing in common*!

From: MataHari@Upzydazy.com
Sent: Sunday, Nov. 8, 3:00 a.m.
To: SuperScribe@BoyHowdy.com
Subject: Reporting in.
Nothing important here. Wanda's computer is broken, so I don't have a proper match yet. Terry, you *did* say the story you're working on is just a harmless little feature, right? Those are nice people I'm dealing with. I wouldn't want to embarrass them or anything by being a blabbermouth. It may be a while before I know anything anyway....

CHAPTER FOUR

From: SuperScribe@BoyHowdy.com
Sent: Sunday, Nov. 15, 7:00 a.m.
To: MataHari@Upzydazy.com
Subject: Yeah, right!
If nothing's happening, why are you sending E-mail at 3:00 a.m.? Guess you're not just sitting around waiting for Wanda to get her act together. (Sorry about that crack but you're so teaseable.) Gotta say, though, the folks at the Yellow Rose don't look too competent from here. I'll try to be patient for your sake, since you *are* my favorite cousin. But I have the very strong feeling that you're holding out on me.

SURE enough, Wanda called Emily the next morning while she was still glaring at Terry's E-mail. Hearing that cheery voice on the other end of the wire, Emily was so swept by guilt that she almost dropped the phone.

"So how was your date with Cody last night?" Wanda asked.

"How did you know I had a date with Cody?"

"Why…why…didn't you tell me?"

"No."

"Oh. Then I guess he did. Whatever. How did it go?"

"We had a very nice time," Emily said stiffly. She'd been up half the night thinking about the "nice time'' she'd had. Between disbelief that two people so different could get along so well, and the first growing twinges of guilt over her dishonesty, she'd missed way too much sleep.

Wanda either didn't notice or chose to overlook the nuances in Emily's tone. "That's wonderful. I told you it would work out."

"But it *hasn't* worked out, Wanda. Seeing Cody is just a stopgap measure until George is up and humming again." Struck by inspiration, she added, "In fact, I'm sure that's what happened to put Cody and me together in the first place. George went haywire and goofed up."

A long pause and then Wanda said, "You don't suppose…I mean, do you really think that might be what happened?"

"I certainly do."

"Unfortunately, George is still on the blink, so I can't ask. When are you and Cody going out again?"

"Friday, but that doesn't mean—"

"No, no, of course not. Anything you say. I won't keep you, dear. Have a pleasant day." The line went dead.

Emily hung up and frowned at the telephone. There was something definitely fishy going on here. Sighing, she picked up her cup of coffee and reached for the Sunday edition of the local newspaper.

Just then, Laurie walked out of her bedroom, yawning and shuffling along as if she was still half-asleep. Spotting Emily, she snapped out of her stupor. "Hey, how'd it go last night?" she demanded. "What time did you get in? Did he lay any moves on you? Did you lay any moves on him?"

Emily grimaced. "My answer to all your questions is—none of your business."

"Bummer." Laurie shuffled over to the pass-through counter from the kitchen and poured herself a cup of coffee. "I wanted all the juicy details."

"You won't get them from me."

"Actually, I'm pretty sure I already know." Laurie sat on the couch, curling her legs beneath her. Still in her pajamas, she yawned and stretched. "I took one look at him and I had his number."

Emily felt a spark of interest. Perhaps her best friend had picked up on some fault in Cody that she herself had missed. "Go on."

"His biggest problem," Laurie said deliberately, "is that he's *perfect*."

"Nobody's perfect."

"I beg to differ. *He* is. He's gorgeous and he's got a sense of humor and he respects women."

Emily stared at her friend. "You could tell all that in the five minutes you were with him?"

"That and more. I think I'm in love." Laurie rolled her eyes blissfully. "Emmy, if you decide you don't want him, don't throw him back. Give him to me." She sipped her coffee, then added, "Hey, I picked up Friday's issue of *Boy Howdy!* Terry's got a really great piece on Thanksgiving. Honestly, sometimes he really surprises me...."

Laurie talked on, but Emily wasn't thinking about her cousin. She was thinking about Cody, because deep down she was beginning to think Laurie was right about one thing: Cody James *was* perfect.

"How'd the date go?" Ben asked his brother across the breakfast table. Since it was Sunday, Elena was baking waffles and their fragrance filled the kitchen.

Cody shrugged and said carefully, "Okay, but she's all wrong for me."

"That never stopped you before."

"Yeah, and I paid for it."

Ben grinned. "That's the truth. Did the two of you just sit there all night counting the reasons you're wrong for each other?"

"Nah, we'd already done that. I took her to the Menger Bar and she seemed to love it. Then I took her to Josie's and she seemed to love that, too. Then I took her home and—" he glanced at Ben's two kids, chowing down on waffles and giggling at each other "—she seemed okay with that, too."

"Sounds pretty good to me." Ben looked thoughtful.

Cody groaned. "I thought so, too. But jeez, man, it doesn't make any sense! When you go by hard cold facts, we're a bust."

"Facts such as what?"

Another glance at the kids. Cody didn't want to say, *She's not interested in marriage or kids, just fun and games. She's a party girl, or wants to be when she grows up.*

"She's pretty, huh, Uncle Cody."

Cody hadn't realized Liana was listening until she spoke. He gave her a mock frown. "Hey, this is a private conversation here."

"Uh-huh, but she is."

"I guess you could say that, if you like blond hair and brown eyes," he agreed, teasing his niece while giving his brother information. "And a real nice smile and real long legs."

"Sounds perfect," Ben said. "Have you leveled with her about—" he glanced at the kids "—your *situation*?"

"Not exactly."

Ben groaned. "That could end up bein' a big mistake, little brother. Maybe you better marry her quick before she finds out. Maybe then you can start paying a little more attention to business."

"Sorry about all the time I've been spending in town," Cody said sheepishly, "but what with all the confusion at the Yellow Rose—"

"Yeah, I know. I'm trying my damnedest to be patient." Ben picked up a strip of bacon with his fingers. "One other thing—you're puttin' a lot of miles on that old pickup and the tires aren't all that new. Why don't you drive one of the other vehicles the next time you—"

"Cody," Elena sang out, "you need another waffle before these kids eat us out of house and home?"

"Yeah, just one."

Ben persisted, "Maybe you should bring this woman around to meet the family, Cody."

"Let's talk about that later." Cody had thought about that but he'd also thought about the way he'd deliberately obfuscated the facts. If she knew he was one of the Jameses of the Flying J and well able to support the lifestyle she wanted, that would change everything. No, he had to stick to his plan.

Cody James, simple cowboy.

Emily Kirkwood, perfect—and perfectly wrong for him.

*   *   *

Friday night, Cody took Emily to the River Walk for a boat ride. She'd never been there before, even though Laurie worked at a dress shop nearby. Gliding over the two-and-a-half-mile waterway lined by shops and restaurants, sidewalk cafés and parks, she listened with only half an ear to the guide earnestly explaining how not so very long ago, the city fathers had set out to find a way to control the pesky San Antonio River. Instead of paving it over and ignoring it, they had wisely decided to improve it instead. Today, the guide said, San Antonio's River Walk—or Paseo del Rio—was one of the most popular tourist attractions in the state of Texas.

And today, Emily was more interested in the man seated next to her than in civic improvements, no matter how spectacular.

Cody leaned over and spoke softly in her ear, sending a shiver through her. "If you think it's spectacular now, you should see it during the holidays." He pulled back enough so he could look at her. "Which reminds me, do you have plans for Thanksgiving?"

She said an honest "No" without taking time to consider the consequences. Rather lamely, she added, "Laurie's going to visit her folks in Dallas and she's invited me to go along, but it's such a hassle for us to both go away for more than a day or two at the same time, what with the cats and all."

He nodded, his expression thoughtful. "In that case, I'd like to spend Thanksgiving with you, Emily. We could go to a restaurant, maybe do one of those big brunches."

"Or I could cook," she blurted.

He looked astonished. "You cook?"

"Don't act so surprised!" She gave him a mock punch. Even so, the solid muscle beneath his shirt surprised her. "Of course I cook."

He grinned. "That would be great. I accept."

Suddenly frightened, she tried to hedge. "Unless Wanda fixes us up with other people, of course. It'd be a little hard to explain that we were spending Thanksgiving together when we know we're wrong for each other and they, presumably, would be right."

"Absolutely," he agreed, the light of mischief in his blue eyes. "The very minute Wanda gives the word, it's *vaya con dios*."

"Go with God," she translated. "In other words, goodbye."

"Afraid so." He settled back and slid an arm around her shoulders in a friendly, nonthreatening way. "Anyway, they turn on the lights down here on the river the day after Thanksgiving, more than fifty thousand of 'em. San Antonio goes all out for the holidays. Market Square throws a *Fiesta Navideña* with piñata parties and music, there's the blessing of the animals and the arrival of Pancho Claus—"

"Pancho Claus?"

"That's another version of Santa. There are Christmas pageants and plays, processions and feasts…"

He talked on and she relaxed against the curve of his arm, content just to hear his voice and think about the pleasures of spending the holiday season in the company of a man who was perfect…*ly* wrong for her.

A man who would probably never speak to her

again if he knew she was spying for her sneaky reporter cousin.

She pulled herself upright and away from him. "Well," she said, striving for coolness, "that all sounds wonderful, but we'll just have to see how it works out."

He looked puzzled, then shrugged. "Exactly. We'll just have to wait and see."

The barge scraped against its mooring a few minutes later and they joined the throng shuffling off the boat. Somehow they never seemed to get back the unity they'd felt for those too-brief moments cruising through a watery wonderland.

At her front door, he pulled her into his arms, being careful to hold her loosely when he wanted to crush her against him. Didn't want to scare her off. "I had a great time," he said, which was the truth.

"Me, too." She put her hands on his arms but didn't push him away, although a warning glint appeared in her eyes. "We can't make too much of it, though."

"Of course not. About Thanksgiving—"

"Don't you have family you should be with?"

"I have family, but they see me all the time. How about your family?"

"My father's dead, and my mother…" He saw the light in her eyes dim. "We haven't seen each other for years. She lives in London with her second husband."

"I'm sorry."

"It's nothing to worry about."

Her grip on his arms tightened and he knew she

was about to push him away, so he leaned down and kissed her. Which was where he'd been heading all along, curious to find out if he'd been right about the impact of the first kiss they'd shared.

He found out in a flash that the answer was a resounding *yes*! Her lips were just as soft, her body just as enticing, her response just as obvious, even when she stepped back to glare at him.

"Don't *do* that!" she exclaimed.

"Why not?" He feigned innocence but he knew very well why not; because every time they touched, it had an incendiary effect on them both.

"Because this isn't going anywhere and we both know it."

Gotcha! "That's a big surprise, coming from a woman who's just out for fun and games. I consider kissing you to be a helluva lot of fun."

She looked startled. "What makes you think—oh!" She'd obviously just remembered what she'd written on the questionnaire. She lifted her chin. "I don't have to explain myself to you."

"You sure don't."

"We're just marking time," she argued, explaining herself to him. "In the meantime, I don't want our relationship to get…sticky."

"Sticky." He resisted an urge to laugh. As far as he was concerned, it was already sticky. "Whatever you say, Emily. And to prove there are no hard feelings, how about I take you to the Alamo tomorrow."

She pressed back against her door. "Bad idea. We've seen too much of each other as it is."

He tried for a mournful expression. "Then there *are* hard feelings."

"Certainly not."

"In that case, I'll pick you up at one."

"Cody—"

He dropped a kiss on the tip of her nose. "You know you want to. See you at one."

With a tip of his hat, he strolled away, ignoring what she said in favor of what she did.

The Alamo was a Spanish mission established in 1691 in what was now both a shrine and a museum in downtown San Antonio. Like all those educated in Texas schools, Emily knew the story: how in 1836, a mere 189 Texican defenders held off a force of 4,000 Mexican troops for 13 days before dying heroically to the last man. Thus was born the rallying cry of the Texas revolution against Mexico: "Remember the Alamo!"

The Alamo complex occupied a full city block across from the Menger Hotel, where Cody had taken her on their first date. Walking with throngs of other visitors across the sun-splashed plaza toward the little mission church, she felt a rush of pleasure that she should be here with Cody.

They moved slowly and respectfully through the old mission, pausing to examine the statues and scale models, reading plaques describing the exploits of heroes known to every Texas schoolchild: Crockett and Bowie and Travis and many more. Emily was filled with awe by the time they emerged into the sunlight again.

Cody looked as if he felt the same. "No matter how many times I go through the Alamo, it always gets to me,'' he said. ''Kinda makes me proud to be a Texan.''

Emily drew a deep breath and nodded. ''As if most Texans needed any more reasons to be proud,'' she teased. ''But I do know what you mean. That's the first time for me and it's something I've wanted to do since I was a kid.''

''Any more wishes I can fulfill?'' Taking her arm, he steered her along the sidewalk leading around the building.

''Wishes. Let me think.'' They strolled along beneath the lacy shade. Emily thought the temperature must be at least seventy on this perfect November day. ''Nope, can't think of a thing. How about you?''

''Plenty of wishes,'' he said promptly, ''but most of 'em I'd better keep to myself, at least for the present. Let's see—I wish I had a taco and a cold beer. You up for some good Tex-Mex food?''

''Absolutely.'' Slipping her hand beneath his elbow, she smiled at him, thinking that you almost *had* to trust a man who'd take you to the Alamo.

Their next stop was a little hole-in-the-wall called Ramon's, where Cody was greeted with great enthusiasm by Ramon himself. ''The usual for you and the lady?'' Ramon inquired as they slipped into a back booth.

Cody nodded and gave the smiling proprietor a thumbs-up. ''Almost. The usual for me, but make the lady's vegetarian, okay?''

Emily had already figured out that San Antonio was definitely Cody's turf and this only enforced that opinion. Unfolding her paper napkin, she looked at him obliquely across the plastic-topped table.

"Did you grow up in San Antonio?" she asked. "You seem to know it so well."

He gave her a quick, probing glance, then stared down at the basket of chips that had already appeared on their table, along with a bowl of salsa. "I was born on the ranch but I stayed in town a lot of the time with my grandmother after my grandfather died."

"Ah, the best of both worlds."

"Yeah, it was. I went back and forth a lot but I spent all my summers on the ranch. By the time I graduated from the University of Texas at Austin, I knew how I wanted to live my life—and where."

The fact that he had a college degree surprised her, although on second thought she didn't know why it should. Not everyone who went to college was filled with burning ambition. "So you decided to be a cowboy," she mused.

"Yeah, well, it wasn't as much of an independent decision as you might think." He picked up a crispy triangle-shaped chip and dipped it in the chunky red salsa. He looked as if he might go on, then didn't.

So she did. "Cody, you strike me as being about as independent as anyone I've ever met. I admire the fact that you've devoted your life to doing what you want to do. So what's the name of the ranch where you work?"

"The Flying J." He muttered the words, then brightened. "Hey, here comes our food."

Ramon himself set their plates before them with a flourish and an order to "Enjoy!" Emily looked down at the enormous platter with huge servings of rice and beans and enchiladas and tacos. Her eyes opened wide. "Can anyone really eat this much food?"

"Watch me." He picked up his fork. "Dig in. There's no meat in yours, so don't worry."

"I won't." She tasted the refried beans and licked her lips with approval. "Actually…I'm not a strict vegetarian. I do eat a little meat now and again."

He chewed thoughtfully before remarking, "Then why did you put that on your questionnaire?"

She couldn't very well say, *Because I was playing fast and loose with the truth and didn't think it would matter.* "I guess that's just how I felt on that particular day," she prevaricated, poking at the cheese enchilada swathed in dark chili gravy.

"So if I ask you a question, the answer I get will depend on what kind of day it is?"

She laughed nervously. "I suppose you could put it that way. As Wanda said, it's a woman's privilege to change her mind."

"I'll try to remember that next time I—"

"Cody James, you old son of a gun!"

Cody jerked back as if shot, swiveling on his bench seat to see who had spoken. Emily looked, too. An old cowboy wearing a battered felt hat hobbled toward them with the aid of a cane, his legs so bowed that she wondered how he managed to walk at all.

Cody sprang from his seat, grabbed the newcomer's free hand and pumped it vigorously. "Andy, good to see you. I heard you got busted up pretty good a while back. I'm glad to see you up and around."

Andy's grin revealed several slots where teeth should have been but weren't. "You heard right. That cayuse not only threw me, he stepped on me and then he laughed." Inquisitive eyes inspected Emily. "Who's your friend?"

"Emily Kirkwood. Emily, this is Andy Dawson."

"Pleased to meetcha," Andy said. He squinted slyly up at Cody. "How good a friend?"

"None of your business, that's how good. Uhh..." Cody looked uncertain. "Care to join us?"

"Nah. I'm pickin' up some to-go stuff. I just seen the doc and I gotta get back to the ranch."

Was that relief on Cody's face? Emily wondered. "Nice to meet you, then," she said.

"Here, too." Andy took a step back. "Cody, when's the Flyin' J gonna hold another longhorn auction? Ben said it was up to you."

Cody herded the old cowboy toward the cash register, where Ramon waited patiently with a big brown bag on the counter. "I'll let you know."

"Ben said you ain't been payin' much attention to family business these days, said—"

"Yeah, Andy, I know what Ben says." Cody sounded impatient and even a little testy. "Give my best to the Box X."

"I'll do that, and you do the same for me at the Flyin' J."

"Yeah, I will."

Cody returned to his seat but he didn't look as comfortable as he had before. For some reason, Andy's appearance seemed to have thrown him. Hoping to put him back at ease, Emily said, "So where were we before we were interrupted? I think you were about to tell me—"

"Forget about that. Let's talk Thanksgiving."

She frowned. "It's too soon."

"It's a week from Thursday. This is not too soon. Am I still invited to dinner?"

She caught her breath. Alone in her apartment with Cody for the better part of the day? She licked her lips. "I...suppose so. Of course, we have to leave ourselves that out."

"That out?" He was making short work of a big platter of food.

"You remember. If Wanda and George get their collective acts together, we'll have to call it off, even if it's at the last minute."

"Absolutely. But I really don't think that's likely to happen."

She laughed ruefully. "You could be right. It's occurred to me that George is nothing more than an empty shell. If that's the case, I don't know how Wanda could get away with it. I mean, Yellow Rose Matchmakers is heavily advertised as an 'all-computerized' dating service."

"Hey, if it gets results, what difference does it make? Teresa told me that Wanda has the best track record of any matchmaker they've ever had."

She raised her brows. "Really? Then how do you explain *us*?"

"I wouldn't even try." He put his fork on the edge of his now nearly empty platter. His blue eyes were probing. "Just tell me this one thing—what's turned you off so completely on marriage?"

"Experience," she said before she could censor her response.

"According to the answers you gave, you've never been married—or have you?"

She shook her head vigorously. "But I have eyes." She frowned. "Why are you defending marriage when you've been divorced yourself?"

"Same reason you're down on it—I have eyes. Yeah, I screwed up big time. But I look around me and I see how good it can be and I want it. Call me irresponsible, but that's how I feel." He gave her that crooked little smile she was learning to look forward to. "Are you ready to go?"

"Yes. I couldn't eat another bite."

"Are we on for Thanksgiving?"

She stood up slowly, feeling trapped but also a kind of breathless anticipation. She could roast a small turkey, make all the trimmings including yeast rolls and pumpkin pie. She hadn't cooked a full-out holiday meal in years. Suddenly, she realized how much she would enjoy doing it again...for Cody James.

"All   right,"   she   said.   "We're   on   for Thanksgiving."

The look on his face sent shivers down her spine.

The telephone was ringing when they reached her door. When she hurried inside to answer it, he tagged along.

"Hello, dear," Wanda's relentlessly cheerful voice floated over the wire. "Did you and Cody enjoy the Alamo?"

"Wanda Roland," Emily said with mock exasperation, "I did *not* tell you we were going to the Alamo."

"You didn't? Then I wonder who did?"

Emily groaned. "Beats me," she said. Cody, who'd been listening, grinned and shrugged. "Is there something I can do for you?"

"As a matter of fact, there's something I can do for you."

Emily's heart stopped beating. "What does that mean, exactly?"

"Probably what you think it means. George has spoken. If you and Cody can come in Monday morning about ten, I may have good news for you."

"Ohhh." Emily let out her breath in a long sigh. So much for Thanksgiving.

"Will you ask Cody if he can make it, dear?"

"Ask…?"

"Cody. He's there with you now, isn't he?"

"Wanda, sometimes I think you must be positively psychic. Yes, he's here." Covering the mouthpiece with one hand, Emily asked, "Can you make it Monday at ten? Wanda thinks she has good news for us."

His blue eyes widened and for a moment he stared at her. Then he nodded slowly and deliberately. "Looks like we may have been a bit premature with our Thanksgiving plans."

"Looks like." She uncovered the mouthpiece. "He says yes, Wanda. We'll be there Monday at ten."

"That's wonderful. See you then."

Emily hung up the phone, her spirits drooping. With a conscious effort, she looked at him with a bright smile. "Wanda says George has spoken. This may be the end of a beautiful friendship."

"Not nearly as beautiful as it might have been." Cupping her chin with one hand, he pressed a quick, hard kiss on her lips. "See you Monday, Emmy."

She watched him go through a haze of tears.

From: MataHari@Upzydazy.com
Sent: Saturday, Nov. 20, 7:00 a.m.

To: SuperScribe@BoyHowdy.com
Subject: Better late than never.

Terry, it looks like I'll be able to wrap this dating-agency business up real soon now. I have an appointment Monday morning at the Yellow Rose. Wanda Roland says the computer's been fixed and a match has been made. I'll believe it when I see it. :-/ I'll let you know what happens but I have to say I'm heartily sick of this whole thing....

CHAPTER FIVE

From: SuperScribe@BoyHowdy.com
Sent: Sunday, Nov. 21, 10:00 a.m.
To: MataHari@Upzydazy.com
Subject: Duh...do I know you?
Jeez, Cuz, long time no hear. I was about to send the Texas Rangers out to find you. Glad you're still on the case. Just remember, you promised to go out on at least one date and I need that date diary....

CODY, in a terrible mood, leaned on the top rail of a corral holding a half-dozen Texas longhorn cattle and tried to keep his mind on the business at hand.

He failed miserably. Cows weren't on his mind; Emily was. After tomorrow, he'd probably never see her again and that probability did not bring a smile to his lips.

Ben propped a booted foot on the lowest rail and glanced at his brother. "We got some good stock in there," he observed. "That paint steer over on the far side has especially good coloration and a helluva set of horns."

Cody glanced at the animal in question and said a halfhearted "Yeah." The fancier the hide and horns, the fancier the price.

Did Emily have to look so pleased at the prospect of meeting a new guy?

"That little scrawny one over in the corner looks like the best of the lot, though," Ben ventured.

Cody shrugged. "Yeah, whatever."

"Maybe we should just sell 'em all and go to raising turkeys or something."

The end of a beautiful friendship, she'd said. Hell, he wasn't interested in a *friendship*, beautiful or otherwise.

"Dammit, Cody, did you hear what I said?"

"Yeah, sure, I'm listenin'."

"Then you're in favor of going into turkey farming?"

Cody blinked and frowned. "What in the hell are you talking about?"

"That's my point—you don't know. Where's your head, Cody? It sure isn't on business."

Cody scowled at his brother. The day was a warm one and neither wore a jacket. "I got stuff on my mind."

"Stuff like that girl you've been dating."

"Yeah, that stuff." Cody hesitated, unsure how much he wanted to confide in his brother.

"You said she was all wrong for you," Ben reminded him.

"*You* said she was perfect for me."

"That's before I knew she was a damned vegetarian." Ben laughed incredulously. "What you can see in a woman who doesn't appreciate a good beefsteak…"

Cody scuffed one boot toe in the dirt. "That wasn't exactly accurate about her being a vegetarian. She said that's just how she felt the day she filled out the forms."

Ben's brows shot sky-high. "That sounds kinda flaky to me."

"You're not the one who's been spending time with her."

"Will you listen to that?" Ben rolled his eyes. "You've got it bad, little brother."

Cody shrugged. "Doesn't matter. We've been called back into the Yellow Rose tomorrow for a rematch. Apparently, the computer was on the blink when it put us together."

"That's gotta be for the best," Ben said firmly. "Trust me on that."

"You don't even know her," Cody flared.

"I know you, and I know you've been lying to her. What good could come of that?"

Cody hauled back to glare at his brother. "Watch it, Ben. I can still lick you if push comes to shove."

Ben laughed. "You never *could* lick me. The point is, you're passing yourself off as a plain ol' cowboy. If she's been honest with you, which I'm beginning to doubt, she'll be all over you when you tell her you're a partner in one of the biggest family ranches in the state."

Cody hadn't wanted to think about that but now he had to. "You're probably right," he agreed reluctantly. "I guess now that we're being rematched, it won't matter."

"Just tell the next one the truth," Ben suggested, slapping his brother on the shoulder. "Want to amble over to the house? Elena said something about chocolate chip cookies."

"Sounds good," Cody agreed. But as he walked along beside his brother to the pickup truck, he found himself wondering how Emily would have reacted on learning about his little charade.

Now he'd never have to find out.

Emily was in a terrible mood. She'd stubbed her toe going outside to pick up the newspaper, which hadn't been delivered yet, burned an omelette and received another E-mail from Terry.

The day had nowhere to go but up, or so she thought until she poured the coffee. It looked and tasted like mud. Where had her mind been when she made it?

On *him*, that's where her mind had been—and was. Thank heaven that after tomorrow she'd never have to see him again. No, after tomorrow all she'd have to do was forget him.

Laurie took a sip of coffee and choked. Responding to Emily's glare, she said, "Great coffee."

"It's terrible coffee."

"I bow to your superior culinary knowledge." Laurie set the cup on the table. Her brown cat, Fudge, leaped onto her lap and she stroked him absently. "Emily, what's the matter?"

The single word "nothing" sprang to Emily's tongue but was never uttered. She had to talk to someone or she'd go crazy. "Wanda called to say the computer's running again. I'm to go in tomorrow for the proper match."

"And you want to stick with the mismatch you've already got," Laurie guessed.

"No! Not at all." Emily shook her head vigorously. Then she sighed. "I might, only—"

"Only you've told him so many lies and kept so

much from him that you're afraid he'd never forgive you.''

"Something like that. Oh, Laurie!" Emily clenched her fists. ''Why did I let Terry talk me into this?''

"Hey,'' Laurie said with a tilt of her head, ''that's my line. But we both know the answer to that. He took advantage of your good nature.''

"If I had a good nature, I wouldn't be in this mess.''

"Sure you would. It seemed harmless enough when it started. And you didn't have any trouble with that Dallas dating agency, did you?''

Emily thought about her first undercover effort for Terry's Valentine's Day extravaganza. It had all been very businesslike. She'd filled out the forms, reluctantly done a videotape—''Hi, my name is Emily and I'm looking for someone with an inquiring mind and a good sense of humor!''—which was an experience she'd sworn never to repeat, viewed innumerable videos done by others—''Hi, my name is Chad and I'm looking for a pretty woman with a good sense of humor and a lust for life!''—and finally, in desperation, had closed her eyes and picked one.

She'd discovered that a good sense of humor was all in the eye of the beholder, and that ''lust for life'' was shorthand for ''willing to hit the sack on the first date''.

Uh-uh, she wasn't going that route again, thank you very much. Or so she'd vowed until Terry pulled out all the stops and conned her into going to Yellow Rose Matchmakers.

Nothing had gone the way she'd expected ever since. Now here she was, spending time with a guy quite capable of getting under her skin in a big way and about to be matched with someone else tomorrow.

"The Dallas agency was completely different," she told Laurie. "It wasn't fun and I didn't enjoy going there, but at least I wasn't emotionally involved."

"And now you are," Laurie said, her expression sympathetic. "So what would be so bad if you and Cody fell in love? He seems like a really great guy."

"Great for the *real* me, maybe, not the me who filled out those forms. And even that's assuming the real me wants a man, which I don't."

Laurie shook her head in disbelief. "That's what you tell yourself, but it isn't true. You're just afraid."

"Why shouldn't I be afraid? I saw what my parents did to each other—and it wasn't pretty—even before a man with money entered the picture."

"But Cody doesn't have any money. He's just a cowboy."

"I don't *care*, Laurie!" Emily pounded on the arms of the chair with her fists. "Cody wants a wife and kids and he's quite up-front about that. Although I like him…a lot, I'm not ready for that kind of a commitment. I don't think he'd settle for anything less."

"Don't you think it's even worth a try?"

"No, because then—" Emily bit off her words and drew a deep breath to work up the courage to go on "—because then I'd have to tell him the truth, that everything I wrote on that form was a lie and I'm a spy for a magazine reporter. He'd never forgive me and I wouldn't blame him."

Laurie sighed. "You're probably right about that. Of course, you could just go ahead and tell him the truth and see what happens."

"No, I can't. Terry made me swear an oath to keep quiet about this until his story's printed. I don't quite know why, but at the time it seemed important to him and harmless enough to me. I mean, how was I to know I'd meet a man who…" She stopped, unsure how to finish the sentence.

"A man who makes you question everything you've ever believed?" Laurie suggested gently. "Emmy, there's nothing wrong with liking Cody."

"But there's something terribly wrong about keeping the truth from him."

"Which leaves you where?"

Out in the cold, Emily thought. "Tomorrow I'll go to the Yellow Rose, find out about this new match, meet him, go out with him *one time*, write a date diary for Terry—and then move to Alaska and try to forget any of this ever happened!"

"I hear there are a lot of men in Alaska." Laurie licked her lips. "Maybe I'll go with you."

"In that case, Alaska's out! I'm trying to avoid men." Emily picked up the full coffee cups to carry into the kitchen to dump down the drain.

"Lots of luck," Laurie called after Emily's retreating form. "But they can be pretty hard to avoid. They're like bad pennies, always turning up at the worst possible time."

Emily thought of the "bad penny" analogy the next morning when Cody walked into the Yellow Rose. A smile curved her lips. There wasn't a single bad thing about him, nothing at all.

He grinned back. "For you." He leaned forward with a flourish.

She'd been so intent upon the man that she'd failed to notice that he held two yellow roses in his hand, each wrapped individually in green tissue paper. He offered one to her and she took it with pleasure.

"Thank you. It's beautiful."

"Just a small token of my esteem. We got off on the wrong foot—"

"Because we're so different that there couldn't possibly be a right foot."

"Yeah, most likely. But I've enjoyed knowing you, Emily Kirkwood. All women are a puzzlement, but you're an absolute mystery."

She laughed. "I'm an open book."

"Yeah, written in hieroglyphs. Maybe—"

"Wanda says to come right on in," Teresa interrupted, hanging up the phone.

Emily hadn't even heard it ring.

Wanda sat behind her big desk, beaming. Emily took her usual seat, laying the yellow rose in her lap and uncomfortably aware that her palms were cold and sweaty, her heartbeat way too fast. She certainly hadn't felt this anxious when she'd been here on previous occasions.

But she knew why she felt almost queasy. She didn't want to say goodbye to Cody James, which was all the more reason why she must.

Cody presented the second rose to Wanda with a slight bow.

"Oh, thank you, Cody. I didn't have time to pick up a rose on my way in today and I do think they add so much to a room." She slipped the stem into the bud vase sitting empty on her desktop, then clasped her hands before her. "I have wonderful news," she announced. "George has checked all the data and I am delighted to inform you that there has been no mistake. You two are absolutely perfect for each other, just as he said the last time—or the first time? Oh, well, you know what I mean."

Emily felt her jaw drop in astonishment, an expression mirrored on Cody's face. "You've got to be kidding," she said.

Wanda shook her silver head. "Absolutely not. I was sure the other time, of course, but you did insist that I recheck and now I have."

"May I see the printouts?" Emily held out her hand.

"The printouts?" Wanda's assurance seemed to crumble. "I...I'm afraid that isn't possible."

Emily and Cody exchanged a quick glance. She knew she must look grim, but he seemed to have recovered quite well. Still, she must persist. "Why isn't it possible?"

"Before I could print anything out, George crashed again." Wanda eyed the computer warily, as if afraid George would suddenly speak up and refute her. Her lower lip trembled. "Don't you trust me, Emily?"

The plaintive tone tore at Emily's heart, but the truth was, she *didn't* trust Wanda, not for a single minute. Nor did she believe that a computer had anything at all to do with what was happening here. Wanda herself, for some benighted reason, had decided that Emily and Cody were a perfect match and had set out to bring them together.

On an impulse, Emily dropped her rose on the floor, or more accurately, gave it a little toss so that it landed just beneath the desk. She uttered an exclamation of dismay and knelt on hands and knees to retrieve it. In reality, she was determined to see if the computer was even plugged in.

It wasn't.

She retrieved the rose and regained her seat, her thoughts whirling. Wanda obviously wasn't worthy of trust, yet how could you say such a thing to an obviously well-meaning old lady?

Cody gave Emily a disapproving look. "*I* trust you, Wanda," he announced. "George isn't the only temperamental computer I've ever heard of."

Wanda looked on the verge of tears. "Thank you, Cody, but I'm afraid Emily doesn't feel the same way."

They both looked at Emily, who tried not to squirm before what felt very much like condemnation. Darn it, she was right about this! But regardless of right or wrong, the hurt on Wanda's face was too much to bear. "All right, don't look at me that way. I trust you, too."

Wanda heaved a great sigh. "Thank you, dear. I was sure you'd feel that way once you considered." She lifted her shoulders as if a weight had been removed from them. "Now we can all relax and let nature take its course."

"Great idea," Cody agreed. He grinned at Emily, an I-told-you-so sparkle in his eyes. "Guess that means we're still on for Thanksgiving."

"Thanksgiving?" Wanda laughed a pleased trill. "How wonderful!"

Emily saw no way to get out of it. "All right, Cody, we promised that we'd give ourselves one date with

George's 'perfect match', so I guess we have to go through with this. But that's all, one date.''

"One date at a time anyway." His lean cheeks creased in a big grin.

Wanda nodded. "No one should be alone on Thanksgiving."

"Will you?" Emily asked.

"Will I what?"

"Be alone on Thanksgiving."

"I have many invitations, dear."

"Then you wouldn't want to join us for dinner?"

That complacent look disappeared from Cody's blue eyes. Obviously, he had no particular interest in sharing the holiday—or his date—with a little old lady.

A beatific smile curved Wanda's lips. "Not dinner, but I'd love to drop by for dessert."

Cody's mouth curved down. "I was looking forward to dessert myself," he said glumly.

"There'll be enough for all," Emily said grandly. "Cody, two o'clock for dinner. Wanda, four o'clock for dessert."

"Five o'clock," Cody corrected. He shrugged and turned on the smile that charmed. "I like to take my time."

Emily had always enjoyed cooking, possibly because her mother never had and someone needed to make sure there was food on the table. After her mother left, Emily continued to see that her father had proper meals. To tempt him, she'd pored over cookbooks and experimented with a variety of cuisines.

But holiday meals were her very favorite. She loved

baking the pies and breads, choosing the turkeys and hams, preparing the stuffing and the side dishes and seeing the entire production arrive at the table in perfect order and condition. She'd done it many, many times, for many, many people.

So why was she a nervous wreck from the moment she awakened Thanksgiving morning?

By the time Cody rang the bell, she had the food under better control than her nerves. Taking a deep breath, she licked her lips, tossed aside her apron, stepped around the cats and went to answer it. He stood there with a big smile on his face, a bouquet of yellow roses in one hand and a bottle of champagne in the other.

"Happy Thanksgiving," he said.

He looked so good in his jeans and crisp blue shirt, so hopeful in his expression, that Emily felt herself melting. "Happy Thanksgiving to you, too." For a moment, they just stood there looking at each other. Only belatedly did she remember to add, "Please come in."

He offered the roses and wine and she took them, then stepped aside for him to enter the cozy living room with its high sloped ceiling and comfortable furnishings. He paused to sniff the air. "Wow, that smells great."

"I hope it'll taste just as good. Please make yourself comfortable. I'm sure there are football games on TV, if you're a fan."

"I'm a Texan, aren't I? That means I'm a football fan. But right now, I'm kind of in a holiday mood. Do you have any Christmas music?"

Surprised and pleased, she pointed to the stereo

setup on shelves beside the television. "Help yourself," she invited. "I need to see how things are going in the kitchen."

"Take your time," he suggested. "I can entertain myself."

She carried the flowers and bottle into the kitchen, where she put the champagne on ice and arranged the roses in a crystal vase. The pass-through counter let her keep an eye on him and she was surprised once more to see how much he looked at home.

The opening strains of "Silver Bells" announced his selection. She stood there smiling, holding the vase of yellow roses and smelling all the delicious holiday smells, when suddenly her heart threatened to burst with happiness.

This felt so right.

He approached on the dining-room side of the pass-through. "The table looks great," he said.

"Thank you." She'd spent a lot of time and thought on it, using Laurie's good china and her own silverware on an antique linen tablecloth. Crystal goblets gleamed, and she'd arranged miniature pumpkins and greenery and candles into a centerpiece.

"I can take those roses for you. Where would you like them?"

"Anywhere." Impulsively, she pressed her face into the mass of butter yellow blooms, drawing in a deep breath before she released the arrangement to him. "I love the smell of roses," she explained. "I feel almost giddy when the fragrance is strong."

"I'll have to remember that." His smile was somehow intimate, as if he truly would store away that bit of information. He set the vase on the sideboard, then turned back to lean his elbows on the counter. "Anything else I can do to help?"

"Can you carve a turkey?"

"Can I carve a turkey!"

"*Can* you carve a turkey?"

He grinned. "I've never tried. My guess is yes."

"Good. I cook them, I don't carve them." Leaning down, she opened the oven door. Protected by oven mitts, she lifted the gleaming golden brown bird into view.

The awed expression on his face was reward enough for her efforts.

Cody didn't consider himself a gourmet but he knew a good turkey dinner when he ate one, and this was a *great* turkey dinner. The bird was succulent, the stuffing fragrant with sage the way he liked it, the gravy smooth and lump free.

He lifted the last bite to his mouth and chewed blissfully. "This is the best Thanksgiving dinner I ever had," he announced with total certainty.

She'd been watching him eat with a pleased expression on her face. "I'm glad you like it," she murmured. "I must say, you're a pleasure to cook for."

He brushed his napkin across his lips and grinned. "I love giving pleasure." He picked up his wine flute and finished the champagne.

Her cheeks grew pink. "Well, I suppose I should clear the table before Wanda arrives for dessert."

"I'll help," he said promptly, rising.

"You're a guest," she reminded him. "I'll bring you a cup of coffee—"

"I'll bring *you* a cup of coffee."

"*You're a guest*," she repeated, an annoyed line appearing between her eyebrows.

"I don't want to be a guest. I want to belong. I figure the best way to do that is to act like I already do."

Earlier, she'd set cups and saucers on a silver tray on the pass-through shelf and filled a silver carafe with coffee. He carried the tray to the table over her protests and poured for both of them.

She gave him an exasperated look. "Really, Cody, you make it hard to be a hostess."

"Do I?"

He put his hands on the back of her chair and watched her in the mirror above the sideboard. Their reflected gazes met. She caught her breath on a little gasp and he smiled because he knew what that meant.

It meant she was as aware of him as he was of her, or nearly so, for he was about to burst with the need to touch her. With the gentlest of movements, he slid his hands from the chair onto her shoulders. She tensed and her eyes went wide in the mirror.

Bending, he lifted her hair and pressed his mouth against the warm curve of her shoulder. She groaned and her head slumped to the side, baring that long, lovely throat. He kissed and nibbled his way toward her ear.

"Not only beautiful but a great cook," he whispered, nuzzling the firm line of her jaw. "You've given me plenty to be thankful for."

"Cody..." She gasped his name. "Don't do this. It's not right."

"It sure feels right." He caressed her throat with

hands that trembled with the effort to go slow. "Turn your head, Emily. I've got to kiss you."

"No…"

"Kiss me, Emily."

She turned blindly in his direction, her eyes closed and her soft lips parted. He crushed his mouth to hers. He'd wanted to do this since she'd opened the door to him, looking all flushed and excited and happy, eyes and cheeks glowing. He'd wanted to pick her up in his arms and carry her off to the bedroom and to hell with the turkey.

Now the waiting was over. She twisted in her chair until she could twine her arms around his neck. Meeting his passion with her own, she stroked the sides of his cheeks and hardly seemed aware of his hands slipping up beneath her sweater—until he touched her breasts.

She gasped and drew back, eyes flying wide. He asked his question without words and saw her answer; she was his and he would take her—

If the doorbell hadn't pealed. It was like having a bucket of cold water tossed in both their faces.

"Wanda," he groaned. He couldn't believe his rotten luck.

"Oh, dear." Emily jumped up and distractedly began patting at her hair and clothes. She licked her lips and refused to meet his hot, disappointed gaze.

The bell pealed again. Their moment was past. She started forward, but he stopped her with a hand on her elbow.

"We'll get back to this later," he said softly.

She didn't reply. Without so much as a hint of either compliance or defiance, she turned away to let Wanda in for dessert.

It could be the best pumpkin pie in the world and Cody wasn't going to enjoy it as much as he'd just enjoyed the sweetness of the cook.

From: MataHari@Upzydazy.com
Sent: Thursday, Nov. 26, 10:51 p.m.
To: SuperScribe@BoyHowdy.com
Subject: Report.
All right, I did it. I hope you're happy. I spent Thanksgiving with the man the agency matched me with and it was a total bust. There's no story here so can I please be excused? Seriously, Terry, Wanda's computer isn't even plugged in—I checked. I'm wasting my time and you're wasting *your* time hassling me about it. :-(Can't we call the whole thing off—please?

CHAPTER SIX

From: SuperScribe@BoyHowdy.com
Sent: Friday, Nov. 27, 7:14 a.m.
To: MataHari@Upzydazy.com
Subject: Getting serious.
Hey, Emmy, what's your problem? All I want you to
do is what you promised you *would* do. If the com-
puters at Yellow Rose Matchmakers aren't plugged
in... (O—< (Yes, there's something fishy about that!)
Whatever, it's part of the story....

EMILY reread Terry's message, then reread it again.
She wasn't getting through to him, that much was
obvious. How was she going to get him to let her
renege on her promise?

The telephone rang and she held her breath. Sure
enough, Cody's voice followed the recorded invitation
to leave a message.

"Hi, Emmy, you there?" Brief hesitation, then, "I
just wanted to tell you how much I enjoyed
Thanksgiving with you yesterday. Even Wanda showing up at an inopportune moment didn't rain on my
parade...*too* much. So when can I see you again?
Name it and I'll be there."

The message ended and she let out the breath she'd
been holding. She didn't dare see him anymore. He
was maneuvering her into a commitment she had no
intention of making, not for years and years, if ever.

She picked up Terry's message again and reread it. "Hey, Emmy, what's your problem?" How was she ever going to make him understand?

And then she realized there was only one way: in person. Without giving herself time to change her mind, she filled the cat dishes with extra food and water, threw a few things into an overnight case, jumped into her compact car and pointed it north toward Dallas.

A twelve-hour drive—six up, six back—would be a small price to pay for peace of mind.

She drove straight to Terry's apartment, where he'd put her up for the couple of days between shipping her things to San Antonio and her own departure. Laurie might bad-mouth Terry, but he'd always been supportive where his cousin was concerned.

It was late in the afternoon when she knocked on his door. He opened it and broke into a wide grin. "Emmy, this is a nice surprise. Come in and tell me what you're doing here."

She entered, carrying her overnight case. Just as she opened her mouth to explain, the door to his bedroom opened and a woman walked out. A very pretty woman with long dark hair and a wide smile. "Damn, Terry," she said cheerfully, "aren't you even gonna let me out the door before you replace me?"

"Oh, but I'm not..." Flustered, Emily glanced at her cousin for help.

Terry just laughed. Tall and angular and thin-faced, he had an easy way about him that put many people off their guard. "This is my cousin, Emily," he said, gesturing. "Emmy, this is Carmen Rivera, a friend of mine."

A *close* friend, apparently. "I'm happy to meet you," Emily said.

"Same here." Carmen crossed to the coatrack on the wall near the entryway. "Terry tells me you're one of his 'secret agents' for the big Valentine's Day story."

Emily frowned, unpleasantly surprised to think her cousin had been talking about her to his girlfriend. "I wouldn't exactly call myself a secret agent."

Carmen laughed. "That's nicer than calling ourselves spies."

"Ourselves? You mean you...!" Terry had even conned his own *girlfriend* into participating?

Carmen nodded, pulling on a bright red wool jacket. "It was a real kick. I loved doing the video, didn't you? I got matched with a really great guy." She gave Terry a sidelong glance. "If Terry doesn't treat me right, I can always go back to him."

Terry laughed and dropped a kiss on her cheek. Emily got the distinct impression that her cousin was not all that concerned. He opened the door and Carmen gave Emily a little wave.

"Don't go on my account," Emily said quickly. "I should have called first."

"Don't be silly. I know how close you and Terry are. I was leaving anyway."

Terry closed the door behind her, then turned to Emily with concern on his face. "What's wrong?"

"Does something have to be wrong?" Setting her case on the floor, Emily shrugged out of her jacket.

He took it and hung it on the rack where Carmen's

had been. "Thanksgiving was yesterday," he reminded her. "That's normally when family gets together. I'd say the fact that you've driven all this way the day *after* is a dead giveaway that something's not right."

"I hope you don't mind."

"Emmy, you're always welcome, you know that. You wanna stay here tonight?"

"If you don't mind."

"Not a bit."

"I'll leave first thing tomorrow."

"No rush." He followed her into his tiny and cluttered living room. Books, magazines and newspapers covered every available surface and most of the floor. A great housekeeper he wasn't. "So what's on your mind, Cuz?"

Emily moved a pile of magazines off the end of the couch and sat down. "I've been very uneasy about this dating agency story," she said at last.

"Why?"

"Because…" She chewed on her lower lip. "I've met several people I really like. I wouldn't want them to find out that I've just been spying for a magazine article."

Terry's expression hardened. "First of all, it isn't 'spying', no matter what Carmen says. It's more like…going under cover. In fact, going under cover has a long and honorable tradition in journalism." He warmed to his subject. "Many social wrongs have been righted in just that way. Reporters do it all the time."

"But I'm not a reporter," Emily wailed. "If *you* were doing it, that would be okay."

Terry's eyes narrowed and a look of speculation appeared on his face. "You did the same thing for me with the Dallas dating agency and didn't get all worked up about it. What's so different about the Yellow Rose?"

"I guess…" She struggled to find the words to explain. "There was something impersonal about that first agency. I never felt as if what I was doing had the potential to hurt anybody."

"So put your finger on the difference now, if you can."

"It's…well, it's everything. The Yellow Rose is in a converted Victorian, not a glass-and-chrome office building. The woman I'm working with—"

"Wanda Roland?"

She nodded. "She looks like everybody's idea of the perfect grandmother. She's adorable, and she takes her work very seriously."

"That reflects well on her, hon. You haven't said a bad word about her, so how can that hurt her?"

"I told you I don't think she uses a computer."

"That's not necessarily bad, it's funny. What else?"

Emily chewed on her lip again and looked down at her hands in her lap. How much could she trust Terry…really?

"What else?" he repeated, more gently. "You said people, as in plural. Have you met a guy you're really interested in?"

"Not exactly. Well, sort of—only it's not going to go anywhere. I won't let it."

Terry laughed. "When you say that, you look like

you've lost your last friend. Why isn't it going anywhere?''

She sighed. ''We're completely unsuited for each other. If Wanda had used a computer, we'd never have been matched at all.''

''But somehow you were matched and—hey!'' His eyes lit up. ''Is this the cute guy you mentioned back in the beginning?''

''Well…yes.''

''Have you fallen for him?''

''Well…no.'' At least, she hoped not. ''I don't intend to see him again, if you must know. But I wouldn't want him to think I just spent time with him for a magazine story. I may not be serious about finding a husband, but he's dead serious about finding a wife.''

Terry leaned forward, his forearms on his thighs and his hands clasped. ''Did you spend Thanksgiving with him?''

''Y-yes.''

''And you don't intend to see him again?''

''That's right.''

''Then write up your dating diary and use a phony name. Names can be changed to protect the guilty, you know.''

Emily stared at him with her lips parted. What a great idea! She'd change Cody's name and he'd never have to know. Jumping up, she gave her cousin a hug. ''Thank you, Terry, thank you! That may be just the out I need.''

He hugged her back. ''Does this mean you may decide to pursue the relationship?''

''No. It wouldn't be fair. He's looking for something I can't give him.'' But there were plenty of women out there who would be more than glad to try. With that knowledge came a pang of resentment that Emily tried hard to ignore.

Emily drove back down to San Antonio Saturday, arriving home to find her answering machine loaded with messages from Cody. Each was more urgent than the one before.

She'd no more than sorted them all out when the telephone rang.

"Dammit, Emily, I'm getting worried. Either you've gone away without telling me or you're in some kind of trouble. My next call is gonna be to the police—''

She snatched up the receiver. "Yes, I'm here. For goodness' sake, what are you so excited about? Since when do I have to clear my plans with you, Cody James?''

"Since you cooked me a Thanksgiving dinner. Don't you know that spending holidays together puts us on intimate terms?''

Drat, all he sounded was relieved, which made her feel like a total bitch. Why did he have to be so nice? "I don't believe I ever heard that rule about holidays,'' she said in a more civil tone. "As it happens, I drove to Dallas yesterday to see my cousin.''

"Hey, great," he said. "Now was that so hard?''

"No, it wasn't hard, and it also wasn't any of your business. Honestly, Cody—''

"Emmy, I was really worried. You didn't say a word about going anywhere and we were together for hours the day before.''

She groaned. "It was a spur-of-the-moment decision. I'm sorry I worried you, but I'm not accustomed to clearing my plans with *anyone*." She hesitated, then added, "Especially someone I barely know."

"Point taken," he said cheerfully. "Let's remedy that. Wanna do something tomorrow? We could go look at the holiday decorations on the River Walk or—"

"Stop! The answer is no."

"Okay, pick a day, any day, the sooner the better."

"I pick never, Cody."

The silence hummed between them. Then he said, "Is this a brush-off?"

"No!" She tried to think of a way to let him down gracefully, but nothing occurred to her. "I like you, Cody—maybe more than I should. But I'm not what you want and you're not what I want, so why go on? We'll just end up hurting each other."

"Let me get this straight. I want a wife and kids and you're not interested. You want a guy with money, so again, you're not interested. Either way, you're not interested."

She hated to be thought mercenary, but if that convinced him... Even so, she couldn't say the words.

"If I had money, you *would* be interested," he went on relentlessly. "Stop me if I've got that wrong."

She swallowed hard. "Cody, I can honestly say that even if you owned that ranch you work on, I wouldn't be a bit more interested in you than I am now." True—"interested" was a pale word for the attraction he held for her.

"I gotta think about that," Cody said.

"I'm really sorry." She felt her throat closing up and knew that she was on the verge of tears. "We'd hurt each other."

"Some risks are worth taking. I'll let you know once I've decided if this is one of them."

"Don't! A clean break—"

"I'll let you know," he repeated, and hung up.

Elena poured hot coffee on top of the cold dregs already in the bottom of Cody's cup. He gave her a quick smile of thanks and went back to brooding.

This did not bode well for any future relationship with the beauteous Emily Kirkwood. And everything had seemed so promising Thanksgiving.... Remembering how she'd felt in his arms, he groaned and reached for his cup.

Elena sat down across from him, her pretty face concerned. "Was that her on the phone just now?"

He nodded. Everyone in the family knew he'd been trying to reach her and how concerned he was. "She went to Dallas to see her cousin."

"You don't believe that?"

"Of course I do. That's not what's bothering me. She said she wants to call the whole thing off."

Elena cocked her head, dark hair brushing her cheek. "The way I understand it, there's not much *to* call off."

"Sorry, Elena, but I don't confide *everything* in you."

She laughed. "If she said she doesn't like you, she's lying!"

He shook his head. "She doesn't want to get married and she's not interested in spending time with a penniless cowpoke."

"She said that?"

"Not exactly. I said it and she agreed—or maybe she didn't disagree, whatever."

"Then that's that." Elena pursed her lips. "If she's that kind of woman, why do you want to have anything to do with her?"

"Because I don't believe she *is* that kind of woman. Remember Jessica?"

Elena groaned. "How could I forget?"

"Jessica said all the right things but did all the wrong things. Emily says all the wrong things but does all the right things."

"Ye gods, now you're really confusing me."

Cody banged a fist on the wooden tabletop. "Dammit, I'm gonna find out which is which."

"And how do you propose to do that?"

"I'll test her."

Elena burst out laughing. "Test her how?"

"First I'm gonna get her around kids and see how she reacts. She insists she's not interested in any of her own, but to know a kid is to love him, if you're the right kind of person." He stood up abruptly. "Elena, can I borrow your kids?"

"How long do you want them, Cody? Is a week enough? How about a month? I've been trying to get Ben to go away for a real vacation. How about—"

"Whoa!" Cody grinned, feeling infinitely better. He didn't like the helpless feeling he'd gotten when she'd announced that they were through. "Let me think.... How about next Friday? We'll pick Emily up and go see the lights at the River Walk."

"They'd love that," Elena agreed. "You might even let them do some of their Christmas shopping. Maybe I can get Ben to take me out to a romantic dinner, just the two of us. Of course, any dinner without kids is romantic!"

"Then it's settled."

"With me, it's settled. If Emily doesn't want to see you again, what makes you think she'll go along with this?"

Cody tried to keep his grin in check. "We'll ambush her," he teased. "Between the three of us, she won't stand a chance!"

The first week of December crawled by for Emily despite the fact that the weather was beautiful and holiday decorations were springing up like dandelions. Even Laurie was incurably upbeat, and why not?

She'd found a boyfriend.

"He works at Texas Treasures on the River Walk," she explained excitedly. "You know, that one-of-a-kind jewelry store? He came in my store looking for a gift for his sister and I sold him a silk T-shirt. He carried it out of the store, turned around and walked back in and told me he didn't even have a sister. He said he'd seen me around the mall and wanted to get acquainted and couldn't think of any other way to meet me."

"That's wonderful," Emily said, trying to put a little enthusiasm into her voice. Enthusiasm was getting harder and harder to find as the week wore on. To avoid being a wet blanket, she'd been working a little later each night.

Which explained why she was still at the office

Friday at six o'clock, trying to straighten out the bills of lading dumped on her desk a couple of hours earlier. Don had said he'd be by later to give her a hand, but—

She heard the doorknob rattle and looked up with relief. She had a whole sheaf of messages for her boss, as well as—

Cody walked inside, followed by two children with Cheshire cat grins. Emily knew she'd missed him but she had no idea how much until he was there in front of her again. He looked wonderful, and for a moment she just stared at him hungrily.

"You ready?" he asked.

"Yeah, you ready?" the kids echoed. One was a beautiful girl of about ten, with long, straight dark hair hanging around her shoulders from beneath a knit cap with a red pom-pom on top. The boy was younger, seven or eight, and when he grinned, which he'd been doing constantly, she saw that he was minus his two front teeth.

She couldn't help smiling back at the kids. They were absolutely adorable. Then Cody's words sank in and she said, "Ready for what?"

"To see the lights at the River Walk!" the kids chorused. "Uncle Cody said if you won't go, he won't take us, either."

"And I wanna buy my dad a train for Christmas," the boy added.

Emily frowned at "Uncle Cody". "Would you like to tell me the meaning of this?" she asked in her frostiest voice, which wasn't all that frosty with the kids looking on expectantly.

He gave her an innocent look. "You remember. I

RUTH JEAN DALE   105

told you how pretty it is on the Paseo del Rio when they turn on the lights.''

"But you didn't say anything about Friday, December 4," she pointed out. She gestured to the mess on her desk. "As you can see, I have far too much to do to—''

"Please, please!"

Cody held out his hands, palms down, to quiet the kids. The smile he gave Emily did not appear at all strained by her lack of enthusiasm for his plan. "Sorry, I should have introduced these two wild ones when we first came in. This is my niece, Liana, and my nephew, Jimmy. Kids, this is—''

"We know who this is," Liana said slyly. "This is *Emily*.''

"Yes, and you may call her Ms. Kirkwood."

Jimmy blinked. "Miz Kirk—Miz Kurt—''

He was adorable and she couldn't help grinning at him. "Call me Emily," she invited. "You, too, Liana—and I'm glad to meet you both." She sobered. "But I still can't go to the River Walk with you. I have far too much work to—''

"Emily, get out of here.''

She'd been so intent on Cody and the kids that she hadn't even noticed Don enter. "But this order—''

"Will wait," he said firmly. He stuck out a hand to Cody. "I'm Don Phillips. Pleased to meet you.''

"Cody James." They shook. "Are you the slave driver who keeps Emily chained to her desk?''

Don laughed. "That'd be me all right. See, Emily, you're giving me a bad name! Get out of here, girl. You've put in more overtime than I can pay you for as it is.''

"But—"

"Hooray," the kids cheered. "We're goin' Christmas shopping at the River Walk. Hooray!"

Hooray, Emily thought. I'm spending time with the one man I wanted to avoid. The one man who made her heart beat faster every time she so much as looked at him.

God, she'd missed him.

The River Walk blazed with lights and hummed with people, all contributing to a holiday mood. While the two children scampered ahead, Cody and Emily followed at a more leisurely pace.

Cody pointed to the glowing row of paper bags set along the edge of the walk beside the river, each containing a glowing candle set in sand. "This is also the *Fiesta de las Luminarias*," he murmured in Emily's ear. "The luminarias symbolically mark the 'lighting of the way' for the Holy Family."

"How beautiful," Emily breathed. "But everything is beautiful. It's like a fairyland."

He took her hand and tucked it beneath his elbow. "It's beautiful all right, but a lot of it has to do with the company," he said gruffly. "This week has been hell, Emmy. I've missed you—"

"Uncle Cody, Uncle Cody, there's the restaurant where Jimmy and I want to eat!" Liana came bouncing back, dragging her little brother by the hand. "Mama says it's got some of the best Tex-Mex food in town. Can we, please, can we?"

"Can we?" Jimmy echoed, big-eyed.

Cody grinned at Emily. "Can we, Emily? Can we?"

"We can!" She offered her free hand to Liana. "Lead us to it."

As they worked their way through the crowd, Emily felt the last of her resistance finally melting away. He'd come after her.

That should prove something…shouldn't it?

Cody watched Emily with his niece and nephew throughout the meal. Before it was even half over, there was no way anyone could tell him this was not a woman who loved kids. Seated between the two of them, she never grew impatient with Jimmy's incessant questions or annoyed by Liana's airs. In fact, she laughed and chatted with them as easily as if she'd known them all their lives.

Cody was content to remain in the background and let the three of them carry the conversation. Occasionally, he'd catch Emily's glance, and when he did, the electricity arched between them as strongly as ever.

She'd passed the "kid test" with flying colors. Now he'd give her the "mercenary test" and see how she fared with that.

The waiter appeared beside the table. "Anything else I can bring you folks?"

Jimmy shook his head violently. "I want dessert from the ice-cream store, okay, Uncle Cody?"

"Works for me. Emily? Liana?"

Emily placed her napkin beside her plate with a sigh. "I couldn't eat another bite—except maybe an ice-cream cone, if we walk around a bit first."

Liana pursed her lips. "I feel the same exact way,"

she said primly, turning adoring eyes on Emily. "A walk is just what I need."

Cody paid the check and the waiter departed. "What does everyone want to do next?" he inquired. Truth was, he didn't care what they did as long as Emily was a part of the group.

"Go shopping!" Liana declared. "I want to buy Mama's gift. Emily, will you help me?"

Emily's velvety brown eyes lifted to Cody's. "Is it all right?"

"Sure. I don't know anything about women's gew-gaws." He rose, moving around to pull out her chair. "Tell you what. I'll take Jimmy with me, and you women—" Liana giggled "—can go do your own thing and meet us at the ice-cream store in an hour."

Emily nodded. "Only I don't know where the ice-cream store is."

"I do," Liana said confidently. She jumped up and grabbed Emily's hand. "Let's go before he changes his mind."

Emily smothered a smile and let the little girl drag her out of the restaurant. Cody stared after them, thinking that if Emily passed his "mercenary test", he was going to marry her if he had to kidnap her to do it.

They met an hour later for ice cream. While the children debated the merits of the various flavors, Cody reached into his pocket and pulled out a jeweler's box.

"I saw this and thought of you," he said, offering it to Emily. "Merry Christmas."

She looked alarmed. Thrusting her hands behind

her back, she took a hasty step away. "You can't give me presents!"

"Why not?"

"Because—because you don't know me well enough."

"I know you well enough to know what you like."

She lifted her chin. "You certainly don't."

"Wanna bet?" He waved the box before her.

"Cody," she argued, "I don't want you spending your money on me."

"You mean, what little money I have? That's big of you, Emmy, but I know what I can afford. Trust me."

She shook her head violently. "I wouldn't be comfortable."

Jimmy walked up, carrying a huge ice-cream cone that was already dripping onto his hand and down his wrist. He licked at his chocolate mustache. "Doesn't she like it, Uncle Cody? I told you to buy the frog. It had green eyes," he added confidentially to Emily.

"The frog?" Emily burst into laughter. "Is this a joke?" She reached for the box.

"You'd take a frog from Jimmy but not a whatever from me?" Cody held the gift just beyond her reach, enjoying the game.

Liana joined the little group. "You've got to pay the man for the ice cream, Uncle Cody," she reminded him primly. She gave the box a critical look. "Is that for Emily? Open it quick!"

"Yes, open it." Cody surrendered the box. Emily, looking suspicious, slowly lifted the lid to reveal the pin inside, a twenty-karat gold replica of a yellow rose with a diamond dewdrop on one petal.

For a moment she stared at it. Then she grinned broadly at Jimmy. "Well," she said, "it's no frog, but I guess I like it just as much." The glance she gave Cody was shy and appealing. "You really shouldn't have, but since Jimmy helped you pick it out, I suppose it's all right. Just don't do it again!"

Liana giggled. "I'll help you put it on."

While the two fumbled with the clasp, Cody watched with brooding eyes. From where he stood, it sure looked as if Emily had failed the "mercenary test".

From: MataHari@Upzydazy.com
Sent: Saturday, December 5, 9:01 a.m.
To: SuperScribe@BoyHowdy.com
Subject: What a relief!
Sorry I haven't answered any of your E-mail since I saw you over Thanksgiving but I've been really busy. Thanks for setting my mind at ease with your idea of using phony names, Terry. I'm sure I can count on you to use that "dating diary" and everything else I sent you with discretion, especially since—are you ready for this?—I'm seeing the "really cute guy" again. In fact, he gave me a Christmas present, the sweetest little pin....

CHAPTER SEVEN

From: SuperScribe@BoyHowdy.com
Sent: Wednesday, December 9, 9:46 p.m.
To: MataHari@Upzydazy.com
Subject: Out of the frying pan...
Glad you've got the world on a string, babe, but I
can't say the same. My editor just got fired and ev-
erybody's in an uproar. Half the staff's hoping to get
away for the holidays, which will leave the rest of us
working night and day. To tell you the truth, that
Valentine's Day story is the last thing on my mind.
P.S. Lotsa luck with the ''really cute guy''.

YEAH, Emily thought, glaring at Terry's E-mail
Thursday morning, she had the world on a string all
right. Unfortunately, the string was tied around her
neck, not her finger.

Why had Cody come roaring back into her life with
his darling niece and nephew if he merely intended to
slink out again? What had she done to deserve this?

The fact was, after they'd parted Friday evening—
she thought on the best of terms—she'd heard absolutely nothing from him since. And even though she
was the one who kept insisting they shouldn't see
each other anymore, his sudden withdrawal was driving her crazy.

She reached for her coffee cup just as Laurie rushed
in from her bedroom. ''I'm late!'' she cried, grabbing

a slice of toast off Emily's plate. "I was supposed to meet Parker for breakfast ten minutes ago."

"I expect he'll wait," Emily predicted.

Laurie grinned. "Yeah, he will." She dashed for the door. "Hey, why don't you meet us for lunch?"

"Today?"

"Sure. Unless you have a better offer."

"Not a chance. When and where?"

"Twelve-thirty, my store. We'll decide then where to eat. Besides, we've got in some gorgeous sweaters you'll love."

"Twelve-thirty, then."

Laurie reached out to pat the golden rose on the lapel of Emily's denim vest. "Nice pin. Wonder why he'd give it to you and then ignore you."

Emily shrugged, feeling petulant. "It's just costume stuff. His nephew said it was this or the frog with green eyes."

"Even so, it's really pretty. Since Parker works in a jewelry store, I'm hoping for a nice, shiny Christmas myself." Laurie winked and rushed out.

Emily sat alone at the table, brooding. After a moment, she reached up to unclasp the rose pin. Holding it in her hand, she stared at it as if it could provide answers. Cody had not only given her this pin, he'd also given her such a rush that she couldn't imagine why he'd pulled back so completely now. It was…well, it was annoying. *She* should have been the one to pull away.

She placed the pin on the table. If that's the way he wanted to be, to heck with his gift. She'd thought it really sweet of him to give her something with sentimental value but now she wondered if she might not be better off passing the pin on to Goodwill or some other charitable organization.

The telephone rang and her heart leaped with hope. She said hello and waited with bated breath.

"Good morning, dear. Wanda Roland here."

Emily sighed. "Good morning, Wanda. What can I do for you?"

"Why, nothing, except tell me how you're getting along with that adorable Cody James."

"I can't really say, Wanda, since that adorable Cody James hasn't called me all week."

"Oh, my, that doesn't sound good. Did the two of you quarrel?"

"Of course not. In fact, the last time we were together—" Emily realized she was on the verge of whining and stopped short. "Suffice it to say we parted on the best of terms. I have no idea in the world what his problem is but—"

"It could be serious."

"What do you mean, serious?"

"You know, like plague, pestilence, broken bones—that kind of serious."

"Oh, no. I'm sure nothing like that has happened."

"Well, dear, if you parted on good terms and you haven't heard from him, there must be a reason."

Emily chewed on her lower lip. What if Wanda was right? What if something had happened to Cody, or to Liana or Jimmy, for that matter. "I'd give anything to know that everything's all right," she admitted. "I'd rather have him annoyed with me—" or completely disinterested "—than for something *really* to have happened."

"You could call and ask."

"Call Cody? I couldn't do that, but you could, Wanda. You called *me*, so why don't you call him and find out if anything's wrong? Then you can let me know."

"I'm sorry, dear, but I think this is something you need to do for yourself."

"But—"

"I'm afraid I must stand firm on this point. You're an independent woman and there is absolutely no reason why you shouldn't call him. Even *I* know that, and believe it or not, I've been called old-fashioned a time or two in my life."

"I suppose you're right," Emily grumbled.

"Of course I am. Now you just do as I say and everything will work out fine."

After Wanda hung up, Emily glared at the telephone and considered her options. Deciding that she was driven by curiosity alone, she dialed quickly before she could chicken out. A woman answered and Emily asked to speak to Cody. While she waited, she drew several deep breaths and urged herself to be calm. This was a humanitarian call, nothing else.

But she sure would like to know why he'd dumped her.

Elena covered the mouthpiece with one hand and announced in a loud whisper, "I think it's *her*!"

Cody grimaced. He'd had a hard time staying away from her this week, even though by accepting the rose pin, she'd proven to him that she was just as mercenary as the last one. Maybe she'd decided he was too big a pigeon to pass up.

He said a cautious hello.

"Hi, Cody." She sounded breathless, and somehow relieved. "I hadn't heard from you and couldn't help wondering…is everything all right?"

"Sure. Why wouldn't it be?"

A small silence and then she said, "No reason. Uhhh…I enjoyed meeting Liana and Jimmy the other day. Will you tell them I said hello?"

"Sure." Cody gritted his teeth to keep from blurting out information she didn't need about how much he'd missed her.

"Well…" She was stalling. "I guess that's all, unless…"

"Unless what, Emmy?" Jeez, let her go, he berated himself. Don't drag this out.

"Would you like to meet me for a drink at the Menger Bar Friday after work?"

Hell, no, he wouldn't like to meet her. What would be the point? "Sure," he said. "What time?"

"Would seven be okay?"

"Seven will be fine."

"See you then."

She hung up. So did he, hard.

Elena grinned. "You really told *her* off," she said. "I guess now she knows exactly where she stands with you."

If she did, she knew a helluva lot more about his state of mind than he did. The only thing he was sure of was that he could hardly wait to see her again.

The dress shop where Laurie worked was buzzing with activity when Emily walked through the door. She spotted Laurie at once, in the back showing chenille sweaters to a middle-aged matron who examined the soft knits with obvious pleasure. Emily edged closer.

"My granddaughters will love these," the customer declared. "Let me have the yellow, the pink and the blue, all in a size large. They like them baggy, you know. I don't understand why, but they do." She shook her head in mock exasperation.

While Laurie rang up the sale, Emily gave cursory attention to the sweater display. Laurie was right, the knits were gorgeous, but Emily was in no mood to shop. Since her brief conversation with Cody this morning, her mood had veered sharply between pleasure at the thought of seeing him again and disbelief that she'd actually asked him out.

Almost unconsciously, she fingered the rose pin, back on her lapel at least for the time being. It *had* been sweet of him to give it to her.

"Emily, I want you to meet Parker Rice."

Emily turned with a smile on her face. "Laurie's talked so much about you," she understated.

"Yes, well, that's good, I suppose." The thin young man in the navy blue suit pushed horn-rimmed glasses up on his nose, then took the hand she offered. "She's spoken often of you, too."

"We've been friends for a long time."

"So where shall we go for lunch?" Laurie bubbled. "I've been wanting to get the two of you together for such a long time."

Parker squinted at Emily, making her wonder if something might be wrong. "You pick," he said, bending over to peer even closer.

"How about Mexican, then? Or—Parker, what on earth are you staring at?"

Parker jerked upright. "Was I staring? I'm sorry. It's just that pin...."

Emily and Laurie exchanged puzzled glances.

"My pin?" Emily touched it protectively.

He nodded. "That's a gorgeous piece. Did it come from Grozina's on the River by any chance?"

Emily frowned. "I'm sure it didn't, if that place is as expensive as it sounds. It's a gift from a friend, so I don't know where it came from."

Parker looked incredulous. "A very *good* friend, would be my guess."

"It's just costume stuff," Emily protested. "What makes you think—"

"That's a real diamond," Parker said flatly. "I work with diamonds every day and I know one when I see one."

Emily gasped. "That's impossible! The—the person who gave this to me isn't wealthy. He could never afford a real diamond. Look closer," she urged, pulling the pin away until her vest peaked behind it. "It must be glass or maybe...maybe zircon?"

Parker's eyebrows rose, indicating that he thought closer inspection was a complete waste of time. Nevertheless, he leaned down to peer at the pin.

"It's a diamond set in twenty-karat gold," he announced. "It probably cost in the neighborhood of—"

"Parker!" Laurie stopped him. "It was a gift."

"Sorry." He looked sheepish. "It's a very nice neighborhood, though."

Emily didn't care *what* neighborhood, now that she knew it was in the high-rent district. How dare Cody do this to her! Just because she'd told a few fibs on her matchmaker questionnaire, did he think he could buy her with an expensive trinket he couldn't possibly afford?

No wonder he hadn't called her after he gave her the pin. He'd expected her to fall into his arms, and when she didn't, he hadn't known what tactic to use next. And like a fool, she'd called and invited him out!

"…all right with you, Emily?"

"What?" She shook herself out of her dark thoughts. "I'm sorry, Laurie, what did you say?"

"I said—never mind, just follow us. If I know that look on your face, you're not going to care *what* kind of food you have for lunch."

Emily followed, thinking that Laurie was absolutely right. Removing the pin as she walked, she slipped it into her shoulder bag. She wouldn't want anything to happen to it before she got the chance to fling it back in Cody James's face.

Cody was so eager to see Emily again that he arrived at the Menger Bar a half hour early. It took a few minutes to find a table and then he just sat there watching the door and nursing a beer and wondering what to say when he saw her.

It seemed so obvious to him that the gold-and-diamond pin had changed everything. Even so, he still couldn't believe that she'd called him and asked him to meet her. Since she had, it was just one more indication that she'd meant what she said on her questionnaire about looking for someone with money.

He'd been so sure that was another of her spur-of-the-moment exaggerations, like the "Vegetarian" response and her avowed disinterest in children. Hell, Liana and Jimmy still talked about her.

He saw her the minute she walked into the room— and she wasn't wearing the pin. Surprised and disappointed, he rose to catch her attention. She saw him and turned in his direction.

She didn't smile. She didn't indicate in any way that she was even glad to see him. Weird. He pulled out a chair for her and she slipped into it. He caught a whiff of her flowery perfume—rose, maybe. No flower expert, he couldn't be sure.

She might not be smiling, but he couldn't seem to stop. "Good to see you," he said. "I've missed you. I'm glad you called."

"Are you?" Her brows rose in a skeptical arch.

He groaned. "You mean, because I didn't call you? I can explain that." But not before he gave her drink order to the waiter. "White wine?"

She nodded. She certainly didn't seem to be very forthcoming tonight.

"So how have you been?" he asked.

She said, "Fine." The way she said it was a real conversation stopper.

"The kids really enjoyed meeting you last weekend," he went on, feeling a little desperate to get a real conversation started. "They're still talking about you."

"Are they?"

He nodded. "Jimmy still thinks we should have gotten you the frog, though." In retrospect, Cody tended to agree. Somehow it hadn't made him feel better to know such things mattered to her.

"Speaking of the frog—"

"Here you go, white wine for the lady."

She nodded to the waiter and pulled the goblet closer, but didn't drink.

"You were saying?" Cody urged, eager to keep her talking. Something might pop out that would give him a clue to her strange mood.

"Nothing. Nothing important."

She just looked at him, and slowly it dawned on him that what he saw in her expression was disappointment. What the hell had he done to warrant that? He was the one who had every right to be disappointed. She'd turned out to be a mercenary little witch just like his ex-wife.

He finished his beer and slammed the glass down. "You're lookin' at me like I'd look at a rattlesnake. Want to tell me what's going on or do I have to guess?"

"I'm trying to figure out what you hoped to accomplish by insulting me," she said, her voice and expression showing cracks for the first time.

"What the hell are you talking about?"

For a moment, she just sat there staring at him. Then she hauled her purse off the floor near her feet and fumbled with the clasp. Reaching inside, she pulled out the rose pin and flung it before him on the table. "How *dare* you give me something this expensive," she cried. "Cody James, I never want to see you again as long as I live!"

"But when I gave it to you—"

"I thought it was costume jewelry! I thought it was the equivalent of Jimmy's frog pin. If I'd known, I would never have accepted it in a million years."

"But you claim money is important to you—

wealthy is the word I believe you used on your Yellow Rose questionnaire.''

"That's right, *wealthy*. I certainly never wanted some impoverished cowboy—''

"Hey, watch it with the 'impoverished cowboy' bit. I never said I was poor.''

"You also never said you were rich, but even if you were, I wouldn't accept such an expensive gift. It looks like—like a *bribe* or something, and it won't work. I'm sorry, but it's more obvious than ever that we're wasting our time by seeing each other.''

Something didn't add up here. Cody looked at her through narrow, speculative eyes. "When did you decide all this—before or after you called and asked me to meet you here?''

"Why, I...'' She faltered, and he saw it in her eyes: *after*.

He leaned forward across the table, his gaze boring into her—and suddenly, it all became clear to him. "You didn't know,'' he said in an incredulous voice.

"K-know what?''

"How valuable the pin was. A true mercenary would have known instantly, and you didn't.''

"I—what do you mean, a true mercenary?''

"You know damned well what I mean. You said you wanted a rich guy for fun and games, but I didn't believe you. That's not the real reason you went to Yellow Rose Matchmakers.''

He saw something leap into her eyes—alarm maybe, followed by a kind of panic.

"My reasons are none of your business.''

"Wrong. Why don't you come clean, Emmy?''

She turned her head sharply aside. "I don't have

to sit here and take this kind of harassment,'' she muttered, but she didn't stand up to leave.

"You lied about not liking kids, too."

Her head swung up. "I didn't say I didn't like kids. I said I didn't want any."

"Maybe not in the next nine months, but you do want kids. I saw you with Liana and Jimmy. I'm not blind, you know." He tried to lighten the mood. "You're not a vegetarian, either. Was anything you wrote true?"

"Yes!" Then she did stand up. "Look, I came here for one reason only and that was to return your pin and tell you never to darken my door again. I'm going to the Yellow Rose and demand my money back, that's how annoyed I am with you!"

He, too, rose. "That's not annoyance, honey." He drawled the words. "I'm not sure what it is, but it's…not…annoyance."

Deliberately, he leaned toward her. She swayed…swayed toward him, not away, her lips barely parted and as soft-looking as rose petals.

But at the very last instant, she turned her head aside and uttered a little gasp. "Goodbye, Cody," she said. "Have a nice life."

He stood there and watched her go, although everything in him cried out for him to follow her and take her in his arms and prove to her that she was whistling Dixie, nothing more.

Wanda called Emily at work Monday. Appropriate, Emily thought when she heard the woman's mournful voice. I wasn't getting any work done anyway. No wonder, after that miserable weekend.

"What can I do for you, Wanda?" she asked on a sigh.

"It's what *I* can do for *you*, dear."

A cold chill shot down Emily's spine. "I'm not quite sure what that means."

"I *know*."

"You know what?"

"About you and Cody."

Emily almost heard spooky music in the background. This woman seemed to know what was going on before the participants did. "Dare I ask what it is you think you know about us?"

"Why, that he bought you a lovely gift and you returned it. Really, dear, he meant no harm."

"How did you find this out?" Emily almost shouted.

There was a moment of silence, as if the outburst had stunned the old lady. Then Wanda said with great dignity, "Cody told me. He called this morning and said you needed another match, that you were really through with him this time. And I told him I was sure he was mistaken, that—"

"He's not mistaken. I *am* through with him. If he thinks he can buy me with a diamond pin—"

"But, dear, what do you expect when you told such terrible lies on your questionnaire?"

Emily's heart stopped beating. "How do *you* know whether or not I told the truth?"

"Because I know what kind of girl you are," Wanda said serenely. "My goodness, the poor boy couldn't win for losing. You say you want rich and assume he's poor. Then he gives you a diamond—"

"With money from who knows where. My God,

I'll bet he charged it! I refuse to be responsible for pushing anyone into debt.''

"It's rude to look a gift horse in the mouth," Wanda scolded. "He gave you that pin with the best of intentions and you accuse him of trying to buy you. Life isn't fair, dear. Now, about another match. George is up and running at the moment—knock on wood.''

"Forget it.''

"I beg your pardon?''

"I don't want another match.''

"Cody said you'd say that," Wanda confided. "He said you were still...what were his words? 'Hung up on him' is, I believe, how he phrased it.''

"I am *not* hung up on Cody James.''

"In my professional opinion," Wanda said, "you are. But if you want another match, I'll be more than happy—well, I won't actually be *happy*, but I'll run the data through again and—''

"Don't. Please don't. You'd be wasting your time." *And mine, and any poor guy who got tangled up with me.*

"It's my job," Wanda said with dignity. "Besides, I wouldn't want my two favorite clients to end up miserable because I goofed—on the outside chance that I did.''

"I'll blame it on George," Emily offered.

Wanda sighed. "Doesn't matter. It's my record that's besmirched. But don't give it a thought, dear. I'll contact you when I have a new match.''

"Wanda—''

"Goodbye, dear." All the sorrow of the world was contained in her tone.

Emily put her head down on her desk and pounded on the blotter with both fists. This was not what was supposed to happen when she went to Yellow Rose Matchmakers! Her private life was a shambles, and all because of—

The office door swung open and a teenage kid Emily had never seen before stuck his head inside. "Ms. Emily Kirkwood?"

"Yes."

"These are for you." The boy entered carrying a long florist's box with a yellow satin bow. He plopped the box on the desk, grinned, waved away her offer of a tip and departed.

Emily stared at the box as if it were a bomb. They were from *him*, of course. If he thought he was going to get back on her good side with a few flowers, he was in for a rude awakening. She should just throw the box away unopened.

She should.

But she couldn't. She loved flowers far too much to do such a wasteful thing. She slipped off the ribbon, lifted the lid and pushed aside the green tissue paper. The fragrance enveloped her as she stared at a dozen gorgeous yellow roses.

Hesitantly, she picked up the card. She knew she shouldn't read it; she knew it would be a mistake to read it. Unfortunately, she didn't have the fortitude to throw it away. Ever so slowly, she pulled the card from the small envelope.

"I'm sorry, Emily," she read. "I didn't mean to insult you. Will you give me another chance? Cody. P.S. I'm not going to give up until I get my way, so why don't you save us both time and grief by giving in now?''

Never! She might accept his roses—she had to put the poor little things in water after all—but she would never accept him.

At home that night, she received another flower delivery just like the first one. Again, she put them in water vowing to ignore the almost overwhelming urge to call him up and scream at him to stop torturing her.

Laurie saw it in an entirely different way. ''Ummm,'' she said, burying her nose in the beautiful blooms, ''this *is* romantic. Why don't you put him out of his misery, Emily?''

''You mean by shooting him? That's a little extreme, don't you think?''

''I don't mean by shooting him! I mean by taking him back.''

''I never had him in the first place, so I can't take him back.''

Laurie considered. ''Okay, maybe, but you want him. You can't deny that. Not to me, you can't.''

Emily longed to deny it; oh, how she longed to deny it! But Laurie was right. She did want Cody.

Well, you couldn't have everything you wanted in life. He was a menace to her well-ordered existence and he wasn't going to worm his way back into her good graces with a few flowers.

Or even with a lot of flowers.

Every day that week, he sent a dozen long-stemmed yellow roses to her at work and another dozen to her at home. She couldn't begin to imagine what this was costing him. If he didn't stop soon, the bill would probably rival what he'd paid for the rose pin.

Friday noon, she called him from work. A woman answered.

"Uhh, this is Emily Kirkwood. I'm a friend of—"

"Oh, sure, Emily, I know who you are. I'm Elena James, Cody's sister-in-law."

"Liana and Jimmy's mother? I met them and they're wonderful kids."

"Thanks. I like them." Elena's laughter sounded proud. "Are you looking for Cody? I'm afraid he's out in the cattle pens. I'll tell him you called, okay?"

"Yes, but maybe you could give him a message for me?"

"Sure. Let me grab a pen—"

"You don't need to write this down. Just tell him to stop sending the flowers, that they're not doing any good except to put him in the poorhouse."

"The poorhouse?" Elena sounded puzzled.

"Elena, he's having a dozen long-stemmed yellow roses delivered to my office and another dozen to my home every day. I know it's costing him a fortune and I want him to stop."

"I don't know," Elena said doubtfully. "Sounds kinda nice to me. You sure you want him to stop?"

"I'm sure!"

"Okay, I'll pass on the message."

"Thank you, thank you, thank you."

Emily hung up the phone just as the delivery boy arrived with another dozen roses.

"Thanks, Eric," she said since it wasn't *his* fault. He'd been here so much they were on a first-name basis. "Just put the box over there."

Darn that Cody James!

* * *

From: MataHari@Upzydazy.com
Sent: Friday, December 18, 7:39 p.m.
To: SuperScribe@BoyHowdy.com
Subject: I'll get you for this!
You think you got troubles? Ha! :-(I'm sitting here
surrounded by umpteen roses sent by that "really cute
guy", who refuses to admit we're totally and com-
pletely wrong for each other. You got me into this,
Terry, and if I ever get my hands on you...!

CHAPTER EIGHT

From: SuperScribe@BoyHowdy.com
Sent: Saturday, December 19, 5:00 a.m.
To: MataHari@Upzydazy.com
Subject: *<]:-}}}
And a merry Christmas to you, too, Cousin. Anything else you want to dump on me? Too many roses— bummer! While you're fussing over your love life, I'm working like a son of a...gun trying to hang on to the best job I ever had. Excuse my lack of sympathy, but...

"WHAT the hell do you think you're doing?" Ben planted himself firmly in his brother's path.

Holding an armload of jeans and shirts, Cody sidestepped neatly and kept heading across the front yard of the ranch house toward the pickup truck parked just beyond the fence. "What does it look like?" he called back over his shoulder.

"It looks like you're moving out."

"Got it in one." Cody tossed his stuff on top of the quilt covering the floor of the truck bed.

"But why?"

"Because..." Cody leaned against the truck and faced his brother with brooding eyes. "Dammit, Ben, sooner or later I've got to tell Emily where I live. I don't want to lie to her, so I'm moving into the old foreman's cabin."

Ben looked mystified. "But I thought you two broke up. Elena said Emily called and—"

"We're about to get back together again," Cody interrupted explosively. "When we do, I'm gonna bring her out here to the ranch and show her around— start getting her acclimated, so to speak. When she asks where I live, I'm gonna point to the old foreman's cabin. When I do, I want it to be the truth."

Ben shook his head as if he couldn't believe what he was hearing. "How you gonna keep all your lies straight, Cody?" he wanted to know.

Cody bared his teeth in a grimace. "That's why I'm moving, so it won't *be* a lie."

"Okay, that would be a little lie anyway. How about the *big* lie—that you're a poor lonesome cowpoke? 'Poor' being the operative word, of course."

Cody gritted his teeth. "I'm gonna confess," he announced. "I'm gonna tell her everything."

Ben nodded approval. "Good. Honesty is the best policy. In fact, it's probably the only chance you've got."

"Don't I know it." Cody squared his shoulders. "Yeah, she fudged the truth about a lot of things, but so have I. It's time we both come clean."

Ben's steady gaze was probing. "You really like this woman, don't you?"

"Like her?" Cody groaned. "Yeah, I like her. Hell, I might even love her. The question is, how does she feel about me—*really* feel about me? I figure it's just about time to find out."

The doorbell rang.

Laurie grimaced. "Gosh, Emily, do you suppose

that'll be more flowers? I never thought I'd see the day when I said this, but I am heartily *sick* of all these roses. I feel like I'm living in a funeral parlor.''

''Yes, but it's not your funeral,'' Emily pointed out. She opened the front door. ''Come on in, Eric, and see if you can find an empty space where you can—''

The face peeking around the long, skinny florist's box wasn't Eric's. She gasped and took a quick step back. ''Cody! What are *you* doing here?''

''Making a delivery. May I come in?'' He did without waiting for her response. ''Hi, Laurie. How you doin'?''

''Okay, but I'm sure getting sick of yellow roses. White roses would be a nice change. Or red. Pink, even. Yellow's rapidly becoming passé, I'm afraid.''

''I'll remember that.'' He cocked his head and smiled. ''You're on your way out, I believe?''

''Oh, no, I'm just—'' She stopped, slanted a quick look at Cody, then Emily, and jumped to her feet. ''Now that you mention it, I do have a lot to do…in my room?''

''Right.'' He nodded approval. ''In your room.''

She departed, darting them more than one curious glance. When she was gone, Emily faced him with clenched fists. ''You've got a nerve coming here,'' she accused, firing the opening salvo.

''I do have nerve.'' He advanced on her. ''Emily, I apologize for everything. But in all fairness, you did indicate on your questionnaire that you wanted a man with money.''

She felt heat wash into her cheeks. ''If I never hear of that blasted questionnaire again, I can die happy.''

''Okay, but how was I to know you were just playing around with your answers? I made a mistake. I'm sorry. What more can I say or do? Tell me and I'll say and do it.''

How could she stand firm in her anger when he was being so reasonable? Her shoulders slumped. "I accept your apology. Now will you please go?"

"Nope."

She stared at him, taken aback. "Why not?"

"Because I want to understand why you got so mad at me about the pin." He gave a short laugh. "Did you get that? *Understand*. This is not my usual approach to difficulties. Usually I say to hell with it and go on about my business. But with you, Emily Kirkwood..." He shook his head as if amazed. "I can't just walk away. I can't let you just walk away, either."

"Cody..." She groaned his name.

"Just tell me," he urged. "If you're not money mad, why did you lead me and everyone at the Yellow Rose to believe you are? Hell, I don't even believe the reasons you gave for going to a dating agency in the first place."

How much could she tell him without giving away her true motives? "I went because..." She chewed on her lower lip for a moment, then plunged ahead. "It was kind of like a bet, I guess you could say."

A spark of understanding leaped in his eyes. "A bet?"

She nodded. "I told you I wasn't looking for a long-term relationship and that's true. But because of this...bet... Okay, I had to fill out the forms but I didn't have to tell the truth, did I?"

"Apparently not."

"I mean, what difference could it possibly make when it was just a fav—I mean, a bet?" she argued. "So I bent the facts all over the place. The truth is…" She hesitated.

"Go on," he urged. "Don't stop now. This talk is long overdue. When you finish, I have a few things to tell *you*."

Her eyes flew wide, but she didn't have time to dwell on that. She licked her lips. "A very rich and powerful man destroyed my childhood. He enticed my mother—" she caught her breath "—he *bought* my mother. He thought he could buy me, too, but I chose Daddy. I hated that man, and wouldn't you know it? Years later, I fell for a rich guy myself."

"What happened?" His voice was low and sympathetic.

She shrugged. It didn't hurt anymore, except for the pain of admitting how stupid she'd been. "The usual. He thought I was bought and paid for and when he realized I wasn't, he dumped me."

"I'm sorry."

"Don't be. It was better that way. But I vowed never to get involved with another guy who'd try to buy my favors. When you gave me the rose pin, I thought it was inexpensive costume jewelry or I would never have accepted it. When I realized it was real, I—I saw red." Her downcast gaze snapped up. "What *were* you trying to buy, Cody?"

He met her gaze, his own steady. "A smile. Happiness. Your good opinion."

"But you can't afford to waste your money on a relationship that will never fulfill your own dreams," she argued. "And the flowers! Cody, you're throwing your money away."

"It's my money," he said evenly. "Whether I have a lot or a little, I can't think of anything I'd rather do than spend it on you."

She groaned. "Don't say that."

"If it makes me happy—"

"But it's making *me* unhappy."

"Emmy," he said softly, moving toward her. "Don't you think you're working awfully damned hard to keep me at arm's length? Why don't you just relax and see what happens?"

She stared into his beautiful blue eyes. "Because I'm afraid I know what that would be."

His brows rose and his lips curved in a delighted grin. "Could Wanda be right? Could we be meant for each other?"

"Don't even go there. There are…things…standing between us that you know nothing about."

"I know enough."

"You don't." She shook her head furiously and held up a hand as if to ward him off, although he'd made no overt moves. "Did you say you had something to tell me?"

His eyes narrowed as he considered her question. "Yeah," he said, "I want to start all over with you. I want us both to relax and stop trying so hard and just see where it goes."

She wanted that, too. But she couldn't possibly have it unless he knew—but maybe that wasn't true anymore. Terry's valentine piece probably wouldn't amount to anything anyway. She doubted her name would even be connected with it, so why was she worried?

In retrospect, she still felt rather vaguely that she'd done a slightly dishonorable thing, but she'd learned her lesson. From now on, honesty would be her policy. If God would just let her get away with this one tiny little transgression, she'd promise on a stack of Bibles that nothing but the truth would ever pass her lips again.

Or as close to the truth as she could stick. She felt her smile building and felt almost giddy. To acknowledge her feelings for Cody, to explore those feelings and find out if they were infatuation or...love...

"All right," she said abruptly. "If you're sure—"

He swept her into his arms. "I've never been more sure," he said. "I want to spend the day with you, show you who I am instead of telling you."

"I'd like that," she whispered, feeling swept away and completely helpless to resist.

He let out a sigh of relief. "Took you long enough to come around," he said, a smile touching his lips just before they touched hers in a kiss that practically curled her toes.

He pointed the pickup truck northwest out of San Antonio on Highway 16. The December day couldn't have been more beautiful, Emily thought, looking out the window in near bemusement.

Everything had changed in a flash. It was as if Cody had swept aside all barriers by sheer force of will. All her secrets seemed to be out, save one, and that one might turn out to be a nonissue. In fact, she was sure it would. But that was in the future. Today was hers and Cody's, and somehow she felt it would be perfect.

She smiled at him, looking so strong and handsome behind the wheel. "How far did you say it was to the ranch?" she asked.

"Seventy-some miles."

He glanced at her over his shoulder, and she somehow felt that he, too, sensed that something indefinable had changed between them.

"Ever been to the Hill Country before?" he continued.

She shook her head. "I've heard of it, of course. Cowboy country!"

He laughed. "That's right. There are working ranches and dude ranches and some that are both."

"Which category does the Flying J fall into?"

"Both, but leaning on the working side. We take in a few dudes from time to time but mostly for working vacations." He shook his head as if mystified. "Beats me how some folks will *pay* to trail along behind a herd of cattle, eating their dust and sweating and swearing that they're having the time of their lives."

"Everybody wants to be a Texas cowboy, I guess." Hearing him talk about his own world gave Emily an unexpected thrill. She'd seen him only in the city, but this was where he belonged. "Does the Flying J have a lot of cattle?"

He nodded. "And buffalo."

"Buffalo!"

"American bison, actually, but nobody calls 'em that. They're coming on strong as an alternative to beef. When raising beef is your bread and butter, so to speak, you don't want to overlook anything that may cut into your cash crop.''

''I don't think I've ever seen a real buffalo,'' she said. ''A live one, I mean.''

''You will today.'' He glanced at her, not trying to hide his pleasure at her company. ''You'll see a lot of things today, Emmy. I hope you take to it because this is my life. San Antonio's just a sideline. I could never *live* there.''

''I'm a city girl,'' she said, her voice as serious as his, ''but that's by chance, not choice. I'll try to keep an open mind.''

''About everything,'' he said. He pointed suddenly. ''Deer!''

She caught just a glimpse of a white tail disappearing into the trees. After that, they rode in companionable silence through the Texas hills.

A high iron gate featuring the Flying J brand—a letter *J* with wings—blocked the entrance to the ranch. Cody jumped out and loped to the gate where he punched in a combination. The gate swung open and they drove onto the ranch, past signs declaring membership in the Texas and Southwestern Cattle Raisers Association, the Texas Longhorn Breeders Association of America and the Quarter Horse Association.

Emily smiled to herself. She was entering a world completely unknown to her. But with Cody as her guide, she hadn't a single qualm.

She soon understood the need for the gate, since ranch animals and wild animals wandered at will on both sides of the dusty road and occasionally across it. The famous Texas longhorns of legend intrigued her with their colorful hides and huge horns.

He saw her interest and grinned. "Yeah," he said, although she hadn't asked a question, "longhorns are just about as ornery as they look."

"What do you do with them?"

"Let dudes run 'em around in circles, mostly. We also rent 'em out for movies and television—been a lot of film companies that stayed here to shoot stampedes and commercials and the like. We have auctions from time to time to sell them to other breeders."

"I had no idea. I thought all the cattle on ranches were just raised for beef."

"A longhorn makes for tough eating, but it can be done. We have other cattle breeds on other parts of the ranch that fill that bill."

They'd been driving along a narrow dirt road full of ruts. In the distance, a dust plume announced oncoming traffic. Cody pulled to the far right-hand side of the road, and a couple of minutes later, a dirty blue pickup careered past. The driver waved but didn't slow down.

Cody waved back. "That's the handyman," he explained. "It takes a full-time employee to keep up with ranch repairs."

A wooden sign on the side of the road said Airfield with an arrow beneath it pointing to the left. Emily laughed incredulously. "Is that a joke?"

Cody kept his eyes on the road. "Nope. It's just a small airfield, though. Nothing to get excited about."

Emily raised her brows. "The owners of this place must have some bucks, then. They must be nice people, too, to be able to keep someone as conscientious as you working for them.''

"I'll pass that word along,'' he said with a wry grin. ''Anyway, up ahead are a few of the cabins where we put paying guests and visitors. Ahead on the left...'' He gave her a slanted glance. ''That log cabin over there is my place.''

"Really?'' She swiveled on the seat to see better. The cabin was small and weather-beaten but with an undeniable charm. A huge old live oak tree spread its branches over the shingled roof.

"Want to stop for a look?'' he asked.

Did she want to be all alone with Cody in the place where he lived? She shivered. ''Maybe later,'' she said, keeping her voice noncommittal.

"Okay. Then we'll just be in time for lunch at the chuck wagon. That's where we feed guests and cowboys and anybody else who happens to wander past. After that, I thought I'd take you out to meet Nickel up close and personal.''

"Nickel's the buffalo, right?''

"Right. He was an orphan and we raised him from a calf. He gets a little confused now and again, thinks he's a lapdog and tries to crawl into the vehicles.'' He pulled into a graveled parking lot before a long, low structure with a huge pile of animal horns on one side of a door and a sign on the other: Chuck Wagon. Parking behind a huge Greyhound bus, he turned to her. ''Be forewarned. Everybody who works here will be looking you over. Think you can handle it?''

"They know about me?'' Taken aback, she frowned. ''*What* do they know about me?''

"They know that if they mess with you, they'll

have me to answer to.'' He winked and threw open his door. ''Hey, you had to face them sooner or later. I faced your roommate, didn't I? Same thing.''

Yes, she thought, climbing down out of the high cab, but there's only one of Laurie and she took a single look at you and declared you perfect. How am I going to live up to that?

Cody couldn't believe how protective he felt about letting anyone get close to Emily. It wasn't that he was afraid they'd scare her off...exactly. Maybe he felt that way because he'd had so little time with her that he didn't want anyone getting into his space. Nor did he want anyone giving away his secrets, but that wasn't likely. Everybody worked side by side at the Flying J with little distinction between owners and hands.

No sooner had they walked through the door than the first cowboy ambled up, ostensibly on his way out. ''Howdy, Cody, who's your friend?''

Cody tried not to glare. ''Emily Kirkwood, meet Jim Travers.''

Jim ducked his head and twirled his hat between big hands. ''Pleased to meet you, ma'am.''

''Pleased to meet you, ma'am'' with an appropriately ingratiating smile seemed the order of the day as three other cowboys strolled past. Emily seemed almost bemused as she returned their greetings. Pride swelled Cody's chest. She knew they were looking her over but she handled the situation with aplomb.

Finally, they reached the service counter where Maude Halper and three youthful assistants dished up the food: good Texas barbecue beef, coleslaw, overcooked green beans, golden corn bread and a big glass of iced tea. By the time they'd carried their trays to one of the long picnic tables covered with a vinyl cloth, the bus was beginning to load. The crowd thinned out, leaving only those who worked at the Flying J.

Emily removed her dishes from the tray and arranged her silverware on the paper napkin. Curiously, she checked out the bottles and jars in the middle of the table: hot vinegared peppers, hot sauce, steak sauce, honey. She gave him a smiling glance before picking up her fork. "This looks great," she said, poking at the slices of beef in a zesty red sauce.

"I'm surprised to hear that from a vegetarian." He'd meant to tease her, then realized too late that it might sound critical. "Oops," he added, "I didn't mean—"

She laughed. "Relax. I was a vegetarian yesterday." She chewed blissfully. "Mmmm, this is really good."

"I'm glad." He picked up his own fork. "I'm also sorry—sorry I reminded either of us of the *q* word."

"You know," she said, buttering her corn bread, "this would all have been much easier if we'd met in some other way. Like, for instance, if you'd come into A&B Construction about building something, or I'd come out here on a bus to relive the Wild West. As it is, we know both too much and too little about each other."

"I'd agree, except we might never have met at all if we'd depended on fate."

His gaze caught hers and held. She answered quietly and surely. "If we were meant to meet, we would have."

He drew in a quick breath. "Then we'd have met," he said with absolute assurance, "because—"

"I thought you'd never get here, Cody." Elena rushed up to stand beside their table. She smiled at Emily. "Hi. I'm Elena James, Cody's favorite sister-in-law."

"Cody's only sister-in-law," he put in, as he knew she expected him to do.

"Maybe so, but he adores me." Elena flashed her smile at him, then turned back to Emily. "We've spoken briefly on the telephone a time or two."

"I'm Emily—"

"I know." Elena bumped Cody to get him to shift on the bench so she could sit beside him. "The kids told me all about you. They're crazy about you, by the way."

"I'm crazy about them, too. They're very nice kids." Emily's gaze lifted and her eyes widened.

Cody wanted to groan. Without looking, he was sure other members of the family had arrived. Elena quickly confirmed this.

"What are you kids doing here? Didn't I tell you—"

"Ah, Mama, we want to see Emily," Liana pleaded.

Emily grinned and patted the bench beside her. "Emily wants to see them, too. Come sit down, Liana—you, too, Jimmy."

Elena frowned. "Are you sure you want to be bothered with kids? Cody…?"

What could he say? With Emily beaming at the

children, he couldn't very well tell them to take a hike after he'd made such a big point about liking and wanting children. He wanted to, though. Much as he loved his family, he wanted to.

"There you all are."

Jeez, now Ben had joined the party. Cody scowled at his brother, who didn't take the hint.

"I'm Cody's brother, Ben," he said to Emily, squeezing in between his wife and his brother on the bench. "I've been looking forward to meeting you, Emily, ever since I found out that vegetarian stuff was just a joke."

Emily looked startled but then she laughed.

Her sense of humor was intact anyway. Now if they could just get out of here before somebody spilled the beans...

Emily had no idea why Cody had suddenly gotten so quiet but she was so enthralled with his family that she didn't worry too much about it. The children were adorable, but she found herself watching Ben and Elena especially.

The way they looked at each other sent chills down Emily's spine. Here was a couple who truly loved one another and it showed. If she had grown up knowing this kind of marriage—

She pulled such thoughts up short. Cody might be looking for a permanent relationship, but *she* wasn't. Maybe someday... But Cody wouldn't be around someday, she reminded herself. He wanted what his brother had—she saw it in his eyes—and he wanted it *now*. Could she give him that, even if she tried?

Cody pushed away the empty plate that had held

his dessert, a chunk of spice cake. "Hate to break this up," he said, not sounding as if he hated it at all, "but Emily and I have places to go and critters to see."

Liana squealed and bounced up and down on her seat. "Are you going to take her to see Nickel? Can I go?"

"Me, too! Me, too!" Jimmy shouted. "Can I, Uncle Cody?"

Uncle Cody gave them a mock ferocious glare. "No! I'll take you tomorrow if you like."

Liana pouted. "I want to go with Emily."

Elena rose. "That's enough," she ordered in a no-nonsense tone. "We've already taken up enough of Emily's time." She shooed them to their feet. "Time to go home and take care of your chores anyway."

"But, Mama!"

Ben joined in. "You heard your mama. Now scoot."

Emily hugged Liana. "We'll see each other again soon."

"Promise?"

Emily lifted her gaze to Cody, who was observing the scene with a slight smile on his lips. "Promise," she said.

Liana wasn't entirely convinced. "Does that mean you're gonna marry Uncle Cody and come live on the Flying J with us?"

A stunned silence greeted her question. Then into the void, Cody said, "Stranger things have happened, cupcake. Stranger things have happened...."

Following him outside, Emily couldn't think of

any. What could be stranger than the thought of marrying this handsome cowboy?

What could be more wonderful...?

After Cody traded the pickup for an open Jeep and loaded up a gunnysack full of dried corn, they rattled on down the dirt road. At the first gate, she jumped out and opened it, he drove through, then she refastened the gate and climbed aboard again.

He rewarded her with a warm smile. "Good work," he said. "First rule on the ranch—if you open it, close it after you. We've got so much stock wandering all over the place that it could be a real disaster if anyone forgot."

She looked around at the brushy mesquite trees and rolling terrain. "So what's in this pasture?" she asked.

He pointed. "Take a look."

They rounded a curve and she caught her breath at the sight of a small herd of buffalo lazing beside a pond. At the sight of the Jeep, the great furry beasts lunged to their feet and stood there snorting and watching the interlopers with more curiosity than fear.

"They're enormous," Emily whispered, hanging on to the hand bar on the dashboard. "I didn't realize how *big* they get."

"Up to two thousand pounds or more—a solid ton of muscle."

He pulled up and killed the engine so they could sit and watch the shaggy creatures. After a few minutes, he reached across the space between them and slid his hand over her neck beneath her hair. He smiled and pulled her toward him. "I've been wanting to put my arms around you all morning,'' he said in a husky voice.

She laughed nervously. "Is this a good time, with a dozen buffalo watching?"

"Buffalo won't tell."

He claimed her mouth. With a sigh, she surrendered. She, too, had wanted this—desperately.

But the feelings he aroused so easily frightened her because they seemed so out of control. Gasping, she pulled away, although not out of his embrace. Her frantic gaze settled on the buffalo. "Are they tame?" she asked as if their conversation had not been interrupted by a soul-shattering kiss.

He nuzzled her ear. "Not hardly. Certainly not in the same way domestic cattle are."

His warm breath made her shiver. "They don't seem to mind us being so close," she said in a throaty voice.

"They're used to us driving around to check on them. Don't let them kid you, sweetheart. You can never trust a buffalo."

"W-why not?"

"They're unpredictable. They're also so nearsighted that they'll charge anything that moves. Trust me, you don't want to be—"

A rumbling sound penetrated Emily's consciousness. She looked over his shoulder and gave a little yelp. "We're being charged by a buffalo!" she shrieked. "Do something! Start the engine! Get us out of here!"

She had no idea what he found so funny until he said, "Emily, meet Nickel."

Looking into the shiny eyes of a full-grown buffalo,

Emily felt half-hysterical laughter bubble up in her
throat—which lasted until Nickel tried to climb into
the Jeep.

From: MataHari@Upzydazy.com
Sent: Sunday, December 20, 11:00 a.m.
To: SuperScribe@BoyHowdy.com
Subject: Walking on air.
Saturday was the most wonderful day of my life. I
met a buffalo up close and personal and—Terry, I
think I'm falling in love. It's the "really cute guy" I
told you about. I wish you could be as happy as I am.
I wish everybody could be as happy as I am! Just
think, if you hadn't forced me to spy for you, I never
would have met him....

CHAPTER NINE

From: MataHari@Upzydazy.com
Sent: Monday, December 21, 7:51 p.m.
To: SuperScribe@BoyHowdy.com
Subject: Where *are* you?
Hey, Terry, did you get my Sunday E-mail? I know I was hyperventilating and I hope you weren't offended. I realize things aren't going so well for you at the moment and I should have asked first thing how the job is going....

From: MataHari@Upzydazy.com
Sent: Tuesday, December 22, 6:42 p.m.
To: SuperScribe@BoyHowdy.com
Subject: Anxious.
Terry, are you all right? I called your office today and some woman told me you were on assignment, but I know you always have your laptop with you so you must be getting your E-mail. I'm going to be very unhappy if I don't hear from you by Christmas. :-(Oh, and by the way, I'm going to spend Christmas Eve with you-know-who. He's really a wonderful guy....

From: SuperScribe@BoyHowdy.com
Sent: Tuesday, December 22, 11:03 p.m.
To: MataHari@Upzydazy.com
Subject: Blah, blah, blah...

Okay, you tracked me down. I'm in Corpus Christi on assignment, which means I've still got a job—barely. The new editor is a—rhymes with "dastard". Nobody knows *what* he wants. Glad your love life's picked up and *one* of us is happy. Now I guess I can stop feeling guilty about twisting your arm....

EMILY only worked a half day Thursday, Christmas Eve, so she was waiting at the apartment when Cody arrived a few minutes after six. She flew into his arms, and when he kissed her, she kissed him back without reservations.

Everything had changed since the day he took her to visit the Flying J. It was as if her determination to erect barriers between them had finally become too much effort to maintain. All those barriers had cracked on that day and crumbled completely in the days since.

Cody broke off the kiss and lifted his head to look around. "Is Laurie here?"

"No. She left for Dallas this morning. It's just me...and you."

He groaned, his arms closing more tightly around her. Burying his face in her hair, he gulped in a deep breath. "Talk about temptation! How much can a man stand, honey?"

She liked it when he called her that. Shyly, she kissed his tight jaw. "I trust you completely," she teased.

"You shouldn't. *I* don't trust me a lick." He brushed his fingers across her lips in a caress before releasing her. "The apartment looks great."

"Thanks." She and Laurie had put up a small tree

and hung red Christmas balls everywhere. A large pine wreath affixed to the wall behind the couch perfumed the air.

Emily chewed on her lower lip, thinking that tonight would indeed be difficult. It was such a long way for Cody to drive for just a few hours....

"Take off your coat," she suggested, "while I get the champagne and glasses. I also made salsa and got chips. Later we can broil steaks and—"

"I don't want a steak." He tossed his jacket in the general direction of the rack near the door, not even noticing when it landed on the floor instead. "I want *you*, Emily. I have since the minute I walked into the Yellow Rose."

Lips parted, she stared at him. He meant it; she saw that in his narrowed eyes and possessive expression. She licked her lips, feeling giddy and overwhelmed. "Cody, I—" She stopped short. She'd wanted *him* just as much and had for just as long. "You don't have to tell me about temptation," she whispered. "I know as much about it as you do."

For a sizzling moment, they stared at each other. Then with a sigh of surrender, Emily walked into his embrace. Once in the circle of his arms, she felt a shaft of pure delight.

Twining her arms around his neck, she poured her heart into a kiss. Intensely aware of his hard body pressed against her own, she felt his increasing tension as if it were her own.

He moved so quickly and unexpectedly that she could only gasp. Before she knew what was happening, he'd scooped her up, one arm beneath her knees and the other supporting her back. Bending close, he looked into her eyes and his own asked a question.

She touched the side of his face with a hand that trembled. "Yes, Cody," she murmured. "Please, yes!"

Elation flared in his blue eyes, but still he held back, although he trembled with the effort. "You're sure? I wouldn't want you to regret anything I—"

"Never!" She touched his mouth with her fingers to silence his concerns, thinking that at last she knew her own mind.

She loved this man. She wasn't ready to get married but she loved him, and perhaps in time she'd get past all qualms.

But she couldn't think of the future when the present was so lovely. He carried her into her bedroom and she clung to him, piercingly aware that she had never felt this way before. When he deposited her on the bed and joined her there, she took him into her heart and body and mind so deeply that she knew even during that act of love that he would be a part of her always.

The telephone rang.

Lost in a blissful half haze between wakefulness and sleep, Emily started. Cody closed his arms more tightly around her, unwilling to let her go.

"Want me to get it?" he murmured in her ear.

"No way!" She shivered.

"No one would know I was answering from your bed," he argued. "It's still early, you know."

She arched her brows and her full lips curved in a smile. "I'd rather not take any chances." Rolling over, she snatched up the receiver just in time to thwart the answering machine. "Hello?"

She settled onto her back again and he laid a proprietary hand on her hip, covered by a baby blue sheet. He'd never felt satisfaction this complete and he was eager to feel it again and again and—

"What?" Emily's eyes went wide and she covered the mouthpiece to whisper, "It's Wanda. She says George is up and humming again and she's getting ready to run my data through again for another match."

He laughed incredulously. "Tell her not to bother." His hand tightened on her hip.

She was his now. No other man would ever know her as he did at this moment. That went two ways, of course. He was also hers and would gladly and willingly spend the rest of his life showing her how much he...

Loved her! Damn, he loved her. He'd decided to marry her before he even confronted that fact but he was confronting it now.

She was talking to Wanda and he tuned in to her words. "Uhh... Wanda, I'm so sorry you went to all that trouble, but you see—" She frowned. "But— Yes, but— I didn't *say* that!"

"Say what?" Cody demanded in a loud whisper.

She rolled her eyes. "I did *not* say Cody and I were meant for each other. We're seeing each other again, that's all."

Cody glared at her. "That's *all*?"

"Shhh!" She gave him a quelling look. "Wanda...Wanda...oh, have it your way! Yes, Cody James and I are a match made in heaven and I freely admit that George has done it again. Uh-huh. Uh-huh. And a merry Christmas to you, too." She hung up, looking a little stunned. "How does Wanda do it?" she asked plaintively, turning back to snuggle in his arms. "Her timing is incredible."

"Sure is." Emily looked luminous and utterly desirable cuddled all warm and womanly against him. "I don't want to talk about Wanda."

"I don't want to talk at all." She tried to wiggle closer to him, ignoring the fact that there was only one way that could be done.

Going against all his natural instincts, he forced himself to remain still. "First—"

"No, this is first." Cupping his cheek, she pressed a soft kiss against his lips. Pulling back, she stared at him. "Do we have a problem here?"

"I want to give you your Christmas present."

Her smile lit up the room. "You mean you haven't?"

He had to laugh with her, although it almost hurt. "I'm serious," he insisted.

She stopped smiling. "You didn't go out and spend more money you don't have, I hope."

"Dammit, woman, I'm not a pauper," he said explosively, trying to establish a little time and space to get his errant body under control again.

"All right." She clasped her hands together on her rib cage. "If you think that's the best use of our time right now—"

"I'll show you the best use of our time." Rolling over, he grabbed her in a bear hug and kissed her until she clung to him weakly—until he thought he wouldn't be able to turn her loose long enough to do what he was determined to do. But he had to. He nuzzled her ear. "Hold that thought," he said, and slid to the edge of the bed. Groping among the items of clothing he'd dropped on the floor, he finally managed to snag the small jeweler's box from his shirt pocket.

He offered it to her wordlessly because he didn't know which words she'd want to hear.

She looked at the box as if it were a spider. "What is it?"

"Open it and see."

"Was it expensive?"

"Dammit, Emmy!" Sitting up, he yanked the box open. "It's the cheapest engagement ring I could find—see, it doesn't even have any real diamonds, just a couple of little bitty chips." Pulling out the ring, he thrust it toward her. "I thought it was kinda pretty, though. If you'll let me, I'll get you something nicer, but I know how you—" He stopped short. She looked as if he'd dumped a bucket of cold water over her head. "You hate it," he guessed.

"Did you say *engagement* ring? But—but—we're not engaged!"

"Oh." He blinked. "I meant to take care of that before I gave you your present, but at the time I made my plans, I didn't think we'd start the evening in bed. Not that I mind," he added hastily, alarmed by the shock he saw in her face. "Hell, I didn't even think we'd *finish* the evening in bed. Santa Claus has been *very* good to me this year."

To his astonishment, she began to laugh. "Oh, Cody!"

"What?" he demanded. "What?"

"You know I don't want to get married."

"And you know I do."

"Marriage takes a one-hundred-percent majority."

"That's right. I figured on changing your mind."

She shook her head against the pillow. "There are plenty of women who'd marry you if you just want a wife."

"Emily." He captured her face between his hands, the ring stuck at the first knuckle of his pinkie. "I don't want 'plenty of women'. I want you."

"Why, Cody? Why are you pushing so hard on this?"

He took a deep breath. "Because I love you," he said simply. "I really do love you. And I think you love me, too." She looked away, her lips trembling. Gently, he tilted her face back toward his. "*Do* you love me, Emily?"

Her eyes widened. In a voice barely above a whisper, she said a simple "Yes."

Triumph flared in his chest. He had her! "Then you'll marry me," he said with satisfaction.

She said a simple "No," pulled away from him and climbed out of the bed.

In a state of shock, he watched her beautiful form disappear into the bathroom.

With her fluffy pink robe securely belted and the collar turned up around her throat, Emily stood at the window and looked out at the holiday lights shining through the darkness of Christmas Eve. She heard Cody's step behind her and turned.

He'd pulled on his jeans, but his chest and feet were

bare. He held out two champagne flutes along with a tentative smile.

She accepted one and sipped. Then she said miserably, "I'm sorry."

He shrugged one sleek shoulder. "Have you changed your mind?"

"No." She frowned. "You don't seem terribly concerned."

"I'm not," he said. "You'll come around."

"Ohhh!" Frustration bubbled up inside her. "How can you say that?"

"Because Wanda and George have been right all along. We *are* meant for each other. Honey, why can't you just face facts?"

"Because…because I'm scared."

"Ah, baby…" Pulling her into his arms, he held her gently, as if she was the most precious and fragile thing on earth. "What are you scared of?"

"Everything. You, me, the future."

"Are you afraid of loving me?"

"Oh, no!" She lifted her head so she could see his face. "Not anymore anyway. I'm just afraid of making a permanent commitment."

"Because…you're afraid you might meet someone you care for more than you care for me?"

She laughed incredulously. "I can't imagine in my wildest dreams that such a thing would be possible."

"Then are you afraid I might let you down? That I might hurt you?"

She considered, chewing on her lip. "No," she finally replied. "I think you're the most honorable man I've ever known."

"Do you believe that I love you?"

Her heart melted and she smiled. "Yes, Cody, I do believe that."

"Then the only thing left is the institution of marriage itself. How about this, then? Take the ring. We'll announce our engagement but wait to set a date."

"Really? You'd do that for me?"

"Honey—" he kissed her temple "—I'd do that and a whole lot more if I had to, but I hope to God I don't. Think about it—you, me, a home of our own, together every night and every day...."

She groaned. "It sounds wonderful, but still... Cody, we don't really know each other all that well."

"I know everything I need to know about you."

"No, you don't. I've...I've done a few things I'm not too proud of."

"So have I. So has every man, woman and child you'll ever meet. Tell you what." He grinned, attractive creases appearing in his cheeks. "This is day one. My life from this moment on will be an open book to you, and yours to me. How does that sound?"

"Too good to be true."

"Then you'll accept my puny little ring—"

"Puny!" She laughed up at him, feeling infinitely better. "I love that little ring because you chose it."

"And money isn't all that important to you," he finished her thought. "I know, Emily, and I respect your feelings. But having money isn't bad in and of itself. It's what you do with it that matters."

"That's not a problem we have to face." She grinned. "So do I get to see my engagement ring or—"

"*Your* ring? Does that mean...?"

"Yes!" She threw herself into his arms, not caring when she splashed champagne all over the carpet. "Yes, Cody, yes! I'll marry you—someday!"

Cody spent the night with her.

Emily simply didn't have the heart to send him all those long miles back to the ranch. It turned out to be almost as difficult for him to get out of the apartment the next morning since every time he started for the door they ended up in each other's arms again.

Only belatedly did she realize she hadn't given him *his* present. It couldn't compare with the one he'd given her, of course, but she'd had Laurie's boyfriend, the jeweler, make up a special belt buckle with the Flying J brand on it. Cody declared he was too overwhelmed to drive after that...but making love to her just one more time would probably help him get his wits together.

Thus it was after two o'clock by the time he got away. She'd have felt guilty if Ben and Elena and the kids had been waiting for him, but he'd explained they were spending the holidays with Elena's family in Kingsville.

After he'd gone, Emily wandered around in a daze for nearly an hour, staring at her diamond-chip engagement ring and thinking that she'd just taken a giant step that would determine the course of her life from this day forward. But the future no longer held any fears for her, she realized, because she felt such a total commitment to Cody James.

She had one more thing she had to do, though.

She dialed Terry's telephone number. He was out, as she'd expected, so she left a message: "Something really important has happened. Will you please, pretty please, give me a call tonight? No matter what time you get in, I need to talk to you *tonight*."

But it was Cody who called her the minute he got back to the ranch, just to tell her he loved her and missed her already. She knew how he felt; she wanted to jump right through that phone and grab him.

The telephone didn't ring again until almost ten. She snatched it up eagerly.

"Hi, Cuz." Terry sounded tired. "What's up?"

"First tell me why you sound like you've just gone ten rounds with the champ."

"Because that's how I feel. I was at the office."

"Christmas Day? You've got to be kidding!"

"I wish." He yawned. "So what's up? Spit it out so I can get some sleep."

"It's about that Valentine's Day story."

"Jeez, I wish I'd never got either one of us involved in that."

"Why?" She knew why *she* regretted it, but why should he?

"Because this new editor is making me nuts. First he wants one thing, then he wants another. The whole project is completely up in the air."

Hope flared in her heart. "Does that mean it may not even be used?"

"It means—I don't have a clue. I've written it, I've rewritten it, I've tossed it in the paper shredder and started over."

She let out her breath on a note of relief. "Not to wish you any bad luck, but I'd be so happy if the whole thing got shelved."

"After all the work I've put in on it? Have a heart!"

"Okay," she amended, "just shelve my part in it, then." This really didn't seem to be the time to tell him that she was engaged. Why rub salt in his wounds? "I'm sorry you had a lousy Christmas, Terry. Things will get better, I'm sure of it."

"Yeah, you could be right." His tone changed. "I've got a few feelers out."

"Great. That's just great. Thanks so much for calling back. I'll try not to worry about that story anymore."

She hung up and sat there stroking the happily purring Chloe. The ring on the third finger of her left hand caught the light and blinked up at her like a real diamond.

She smiled, unconsciously hugging the cat so hard that Chloe squealed and struggled free. I'm in love, Emily realized with a sense of wonder. Life is very, very good....

Cody and Emily brought in the new year at a local club with Laurie and Parker. They'd agreed that once Laurie returned from her holidays in Dallas, their opportunities to be alone together would be sharply curtailed.

"It's better that way, Emmy," Cody said, holding her in his arms and trying to force himself to say good-night and make it stick. "I don't want you now and then. I want you forever. Besides—" he gave her a broad wink "—suffering builds character."

By New Year's Eve, he thought he must have built enough character to last him a lifetime. As the clock struck midnight, while confetti and balloons cascaded gently around them, he held her in his arms and kissed her with pent-up passion.

"I haven't made love to you for three days and it's about to kill me," he grated in her ear. "I don't know how much of this I can take. Are you sure you're not ready to set a date?"

He'd meant it as a plaintive joke, but her response was anything but laughable. "How about June 15?"

He stared at her, wondering if he'd heard her correctly. When she nodded, even a crowded dance floor couldn't stop him. With a whoop of joy, he picked her up and whirled her around, stopping only when he couldn't go another second without kissing her.

"You mean it, don't you?" he asked at last.

"I mean it." She swallowed hard. "I'm still scared of marriage but I'm more scared of being without you."

And that's how the date was set.

The first week of January, they made it a point to drop by the Yellow Rose. Waiting for Wanda to see them, Emily could barely contain her joy. And to think all this had happened because of Terry! If it hadn't been for him, she'd never have heard of Cody James.

Teresa's telephone rang and she spoke briefly, then smiled at the waiting couple. "Go right in. Wanda's eager to see you."

Cody and Emily exchanged smiles. When he held out his hand, she took it and followed him into the office.

Wanda stood in front of her computer, frowning. When she looked up and saw them, the frown magically disappeared. "Children!" She hurried around the desk, arms outstretched. "Does this mean what I think it means?"

"Probably," Cody said. "What do you think it means?"

"That you've realized the truth—you *are* meant for each other."

"You were right all along, Wanda." Emily looked at the handsome cowboy at her side and happiness overwhelmed her. She took a deep breath to steady her drumming heartbeat, the aroma of the yellow roses on the desk almost making her head swim. She held out her left hand. "We're engaged!"

"Oh, my goodness!" Wanda fairly hopped up and down in her excitement. She hugged first Emily, then Cody, then tried to hug them both at the same time. "This is the most wonderful news! When's the big day?"

"June 15."

Wanda looked quite taken aback by this news. "Why, Emily, that's almost six months away. How can two people so in love wait so long?"

"It's not *that* long." Emily looked at Cody for support.

He grinned. "It sure seems 'that long' to me. Of course, there are a lot of things to do, decisions to be made, but if I had my way..." He gave Emily a look of cautious optimism.

"Go on," Wanda urged. "If you had your way, when would *you* like to get married, Cody?"

Emily could almost see him sifting dates in his mind. Then he grinned as if he'd outmaneuvered her this time.

"February 14," he said softly. "I'd marry my true love on Valentine's Day."

"Oh, Cody!" Emily threw her arms around him and hugged him tight. Who could resist a man who said things like that?

A little later when they left a jubilant Wanda and walked out on the wide porch of the Yellow Rose, Cody caught her elbow and swung her around to face him. "I meant it, Emily," he said. "God, I don't know if I can wait until June to have you all to myself."

The merest touch of his hand made her tremble with longing. "I know how you feel, believe me, only—"

"Only what? Do you want a big wedding? Is that it?"

"Absolutely not. I don't have all that much family anyway—really just my cousin Terry. Besides, I could be transferred back to Dallas any day. If I had my way, we'd just elope and skip all the hoopla—" She broke off abruptly, staring at him.

"Elope! That's it!" Cody declared enthusiastically.

"But wouldn't Ben and Elena be disappointed if you did?"

"They had their wedding. This one is mine—the last one I'll ever have." He gathered her close, bending to stare into her face. "Let's do it. Let's elope."

"But—"

"Valentine's Day, okay? We can worry about details later."

Her heartbeat accelerated. "What day does February 14 fall on?"

He hauled out a checkbook stashed in his hip

pocket and flipped the small calendars in the front. Impatiently running his thumb over the numbers, he found what he was looking for at last. "It's on a Sunday."

"Sunday, huh." She licked her lips, a plan forming in her mind. "We could get married the Friday before and take our honeymoon—"

"Yes!" He stopped her with a kiss.

She pulled back, laughing. "As I was about to say, we could have a weekend honeymoon."

"For starters," he agreed. "Then next summer we can get away for a real honeymoon."

"Sweetheart, any time and anywhere we're together will be a honeymoon."

That brought a lecherous grin to his lips. "I agree—but why not go to Key West or the Bahamas or someplace—"

"Expensive." She shook her head indulgently. "We'll discuss that later. In the meantime, we've got a wedding to get ready for."

From: MataHari@Upzydazy.com
Sent: Wednesday, February 10, 8:22 a.m.
To: SuperScribe@BoyHowdy.com
Subject: Top secret!
Terry, I've been dying to tell you the news and now I finally can. Cody and I are getting married Friday at two o'clock in the office of a judge who's been a friend of his family for years. I'm so thrilled I'm practically incoherent! :-))) The only reason I haven't told you before is because we're more or less eloping. No one knows except Laurie, and now you. I don't suppose you could make it here for the ceremony, but if you could it would make me so happy....

CHAPTER TEN

From: System Administrator
Sent: Wednesday, February 10, 9:59 a.m.
Subject: Undeliverable: Top secret!
Your message did not reach the intended recipient.
Subject: Top secret!
Sent: February 10, 8:22 a.m.
The following recipient could not be reached:
SuperScribe@BoyHowdy.com

EMILY took her boss into her confidence because she had to. Don gave her a big hug along with Thursday and Friday off, even though her marriage would, in his words, "play hell with this office!"

"I'm sorry," she said contritely. "Cody and I still have a lot of details to work out, but he agrees I shouldn't leave you in the lurch."

"Don't worry about that. They've been begging me to send you back to the Dallas office anyway." He cocked his head thoughtfully. "Emily, you haven't known this guy very long. Are you sure—"

"Yes!" She took no offense at his doubtful expression. She'd already wrestled with, and resolved, her own doubts. "I don't blame you for being surprised—everyone who knows me will be. But I love him, Don. It's as simple as that."

And it was.

With Laurie as advisor, Emily finally found a dress she liked Wednesday night. She settled on a soft cream-colored chiffon with flowing skirt and gracefully gathered sleeves. It took longer to find the veil than it had the dress, but it was worth the effort. The fingertip-length illusion netting gathered onto a Juliet cap of pearls was the same perfect shade of cream.

Far too excited and happy to sleep, Emily talked on the telephone with Cody for over an hour Wednesday evening, then tossed and turned in her lonely bed the rest of the night. All she could think about was that soon he'd be beside her, not seventy-some miles away.

She could hardy wait!

She'd made an appointment at a health spa for the following day and emerged from that experience at six, polished and glowing. She'd never looked or felt better—until she got home and checked her E-mail.

Her message to Terry was undeliverable? What in the world did that mean? She dialed *Boy Howdy!* immediately but got an answering machine. Next, she tried Terry's home number but got his machine, too. She left a message. "Terry, what's happened? Why has your E-mail bounced? Where are you? Call me!"

Cody wanted to drive into town to take her out to dinner Thursday night, but she put him off. "Starting tomorrow, you'll be seeing so much of me you'll probably get sick of it," she teased.

"Not a chance." His voice sounded so low and sexy that it sent little shivers through her. "I'm just worried about getting through tonight without you."

"This will be the last one, darling," she whispered.

"Starting tomorrow, we'll be together always. I promise…"

Cody skipped breakfast Friday morning, then felt queasy because he was hungry. He decided to drop in at the chuck wagon for a bite to eat a few minutes before nine. He had to turn on all his charm to get the cook to mess up her clean grill for him, but she finally consented.

Ben stormed in minutes later. Grim-faced, he threw a newspaper on the wooden table before sitting down across from his brother. "I like to never found you," he said. "Don't you work anymore?" He banged a fist on the paper. "Read it and weep."

Cody frowned over his plateful of scrambled eggs. He'd been hungry when he ordered but found he could barely force down a bite. Annoyed, he picked up the copy of the San Antonio daily. "What am I supposed to be looking at?" he demanded, his tone testy.

Ben grabbed the paper and ripped through it, then refolded and handed it back. Cody read the headline: Ranching Dynasty One Of Many In Hill Country.

"Yeah," he said impatiently. "Looks like a story about the Connors over on the Box X."

"That's right. And farther down there's a mention of other ranching families, including the Jameses of the Flying J. And over here—" he stabbed a finger at a boxed item Cody hadn't even noticed "—is a listing of Hill Country ranches, their size, a paragraph about their history and who's runnin' 'em now. Wanna hear yours?"

He grabbed the paper out of Cody's numb hand. "'Younger son, Cody James, handles the day-to-day operations at the Flying J while big brother, Ben, handles real estate. Running cattle and buffalo primarily, it's one of the most successful operations in Texas, or any other state, for that matter.'"

The brothers looked at each other, one exasperated and the other stunned.

Ben exploded. "I told you to tell Emily! When she sees this—"

"She won't see it," Cody said in a ragged voice. But he knew she would unless he was the luckiest SOB in Texas. She was a subscriber to the newspaper, and she'd be vitally interested in anything that affected the man she was about to marry.

The *lying* man she was about to marry.

"Thank God you've got time to clear this up," Ben said. "The wedding's not until June 15. Maybe she'll get over it by then."

"By then?" Cody surged to his feet, wild-eyed. "Hell, Ben, I've got exactly—" he looked at his wristwatch "—I've got exactly four hours and forty-seven minutes to find her and convince her that I'm not the worst liar in all of Texas."

Ben's jaw dropped. "You're not tellin' me—"

"Tryin' hard not to," Cody agreed, plunging toward the door. "If you're a praying man, Ben, now would be a good time."

Cody raced back to his cabin and dialed her number with shaking hands. What a day for this to come up! He should have told her he was a member of an important ranching family, not a happy-go-lucky cowboy. Why *hadn't* he? She'd have understood.

She *will* understand, he promised himself. She's got to.

Because he loved her. He loved her with every fiber of his being. He loved her good points and her bad, her highs and her lows, and he would love her until the day he died.

Emily and Laurie parted company at nine-thirty Friday morning, Laurie handling last-minute errands including picking up the flowers, while Emily headed for the beauty parlor. There she was pampered and petted. By the time she left at eleven-thirty, she'd been cut and curled and manicured, given a facial and had her makeup done.

She felt wonderful! Letting herself back into the apartment, she made straight for her bedroom, where she slipped eagerly into the chiffon dress. Twisting and preening before the mirror, she realized that not a single cloud marred her horizon.

She heard the front door open, then Laurie's voice. "Emily, are you here?"

Something was wrong. Laurie's voice quivered as if she was on the verge of tears. A shiver of apprehension shot down Emily's spine and she hurried to her bedroom door and threw it open.

"Laurie, what is it?"

Laurie did indeed seem on the verge of tears. She waved a magazine in the air with one hand while, with the other, she clutched a large white cardboard florist's box. "This!" she shrieked. "Oh, Emily, how *could* he?"

Emily's heart constricted into a tight little ball of dread. "I won't know until I see—" She grabbed the magazine, saw the red-white-and-blue logo of *Boy Howdy!* and gasped. No, surely not. Terry couldn't have...

She ripped through the glossy pages with numb fingers.

"It's on page fifty-two," Laurie said. "Oh, Emily, I'm so sorry!"

Emily stared down at the two-page opener for the Valentine's Day feature, scanned the headlines and wanted to cry: How Stupid Is Cupid, Anyway? Trio Of Texas Lovelies Set Out To Learn The Answers... The Amorous Adventures Of Avis Addison, Carmen Rivera And Emily Kirkwood...

"Oh, my God!" Emily collapsed into a chair, the magazine falling from her fingers. "I can't look at any more." She buried her face in her hands. "How bad is it, Laurie?"

"Bad," Laurie said grimly. "It makes you look like Mata Hari, Wanda sounds like a dotty old lady, and Cody—"

"Not Cody!" Emily yanked her head up and stared at her friend. "They don't name him, do they?"

"No, but he'll sure know who he is." Tears rolled down Laurie's cheeks. "I can't believe Terry did this to you, Emily. The whole thing is presented as just a lark, all light and funny, only it *isn't*! When Cody sees this—"

"Cody!" Emily jumped to her feet. "My God, I've

got to tell him before he finds out on his own.'' She glanced at her wristwatch. ''It's already noon. Do you suppose he's still at the ranch?''

''Call,'' Laurie urged. ''He'll understand if he hears it from you first.''

Emily reached for the telephone and only then did she see the message-waiting light blinking on the answering machine. She snatched back her hand and clutched her stomach, her terrified gaze locking with Laurie's.

''I didn't notice we had a message when I came in,'' she said, licking her lips. ''M-maybe it's Parker.''

''I hope so.'' Laurie punched the button. ''Or maybe—''

''Don't even say it!''

The electronic voice of the machine sputtered out, ''You have one message.'' Emily closed her eyes and prayed.

''Emily, it's me, Cody.''

She gasped. He sounded terribly upset.

''I know we said we weren't gonna get all hung up on things that happened in the past, but dammit! Some things can't be glossed over. I've got to see you before the wedding.'' Static interfered and his voice faded, then drifted back in. ''...bar at one...'' Static.

The tape played out, stopped and rewound. Emily stared at Laurie, feeling as if she'd been turned inside out by his words. ''He knows,'' she whimpered, barely able to force the words from her constricted throat.

Laurie put her arm around her friend's waist. ''It

sounds like it," she admitted. "But look on the bright side—he wants to talk to you. He didn't call the wedding off."

"He will. He's been honest with me from day one and I've lied to him the entire time."

"Where is it he wants to meet you?" Laurie punched the Play button again.

This time they clearly made out, above the static, "Menger Bar".

"At one," Laurie said. "You'd better hurry."

"You're right. Maybe I can still make him understand." Emily pulled her wool coat off the rack and shoved her arms into it.

"Would you like me to go with you?"

"Yes, but don't. I got myself into this and I have to get myself out." Emily threw open the door, then ran back to grab the magazine. She'd better look this over more carefully so she'd know how much damage had been done.

"Good luck," Laurie called after her. "I'll meet you at the judge's chamber a little before two."

Emily nodded and waved. She only hoped there would still be a reason to go there.

She reached the Menger Bar with five minutes to spare and saw at once that Cody wasn't there. She took a seat where she could watch both doors and ordered mineral water. She didn't dare touch alcohol or she might come completely undone.

Spreading the magazine before her, she tried to read the Valentine's Day feature but couldn't force herself to go beyond the headlines. How could Terry *do* this to her? She frowned. The article was bylined Kevin Percy, whoever that might be. Terry was only mentioned under "Staff members also contributing to this story include…"

She closed the magazine and sat there with head and shoulders drooping. What difference did it make who got the credit—or blame, as the case might be. Her life had been ruined. Cody would never forgive her. She might as well pack up and leave town.

She glanced at her wristwatch: 1:13. He'd picked the time and was still late.

Because he's not coming, idiot! Her eyes snapped wide. He wasn't coming. He'd decided he didn't even want to hear her side of the story, miserable though it might be. If he wasn't here by 1:15, she promised herself, she'd get in her car, drive straight to Dallas and forget she'd ever known—ever *loved* a cowboy named Cody James. She glanced at her watch again. Yes, at 1:20 she'd leave for sure…at 1:25…

At 1:30 she faced facts. It was over. What should have been the happiest day of her life had instead turned into a shambles. She'd been dumped—again. But she'd also been right about one thing: marriage was not for her. After trying—and failing miserably— not one but two times, she doubted she'd ever be interested in taking another chance.

One thirty-six.

She stood up abruptly. It was over.

She drove through unfamiliar neighborhoods of San Antonio in a blur of pain, trying to find the freeway so she could head north to Dallas. But for some reason, she didn't seem to be able to make her way through the maze of streets.

In a panic, she made a sudden right-hand turn and found herself on Bluebonnet Drive. All at once she saw with stark clarity that although she was to blame for her current predicament, there was someone else who'd also had a hand in her fall. She had one more thing to do before she drove out of San Antonio for the last time....

Cody drove the last ten miles into San Antonio swearing so loudly he drowned out the radio. Ben had warned him time and again to put new tires on his pickup truck, but he'd been too busy to heed good advice. As a result, Cody realized he might very well have lost the only woman he'd ever love.

Pulling into a No Parking zone beside the Menger, he jumped out and dashed for the door. Inside the bar, he stared around with the kind of panic he'd never felt before.

Where the hell was she? He glanced at his watch and saw with a start that it was 1:37. He was late, but she could have waited. It wasn't as if this meeting wasn't important to the rest of their lives.

He stalked to the bar. The bartender looked up politely. "May I get you something, sir?"

"Information. Was there a woman in here alone a little while ago...beautiful, blond hair, big brown eyes, about so high?" He held out a level hand at chin height.

"Sure was."

"So what happened to her?" Cody exploded.

"She left."

Cody counted to three. "I can see that. Do you know where she went?"

The bartender shrugged. "She paid her tab but she didn't confide in me."

"Great." Now what? Cody turned toward the door.

"She did look—"

"She did look what?" Cody whirled back.

The bartender frowned. "Not happy. I don't know if she was mad or sad or what, but she didn't look happy. She was reading something...."

Cody's stomach clenched tighter. "A newspaper?"

"Coulda been. I didn't look too close. Whatever it was sure didn't make her happy."

Damn. So much for getting to her before she read the paper.

"She also kept looking at her watch as if she was waiting for someone. That would be you, I take it."

"Yeah. I had a flat tire and—dammit, why couldn't she have waited another minute or two?"

The bartender looked sympathetic. "That's all it woulda taken. You just missed her by a hair. Sorry."

Sorry. The story of my life, Cody thought, walking back to his pickup with dragging steps. Sorry he'd met Jessica first, sorry he hadn't met Emily before some idiot broke her heart, sorry he hadn't been honest with her—

"Hey!" He reared back and stared at the piece of paper affixed beneath his windshield wiper.

Poetic justice. He'd left his truck parked illegally for less than ten minutes and he already had a ticket.

Sometimes life sucked.

Crawling behind the wheel, he considered his options. He could try to track her down and make her listen, or he could crawl back to the ranch, lick his wounds and forget all about that fantasy wife and kids he'd been so determined to have.

When he drove away from the Menger, he still hadn't decided which road to take.

Emily leaned forward with both palms planted flat on Teresa's desk. "I've got to see Wanda!" she cried. "It's a matter of life or death!"

Teresa blinked and did a double take. "Holy cow, Emily, what's the matter?"

"Everything's the matter and it's all George's fault." Emily stifled a groan. "Look, I'm leaving town. Before I go, I've got to talk to Wanda one last time."

"Oh, dear, we'll be sorry to lose you in San Antone," Teresa said. "When are you going?"

"Any minute now. This is my last stop and I don't have a lot of time to spare so—"

"I'll tell her you're here." Teresa reached for the telephone. "Wanda, Emily Kirkwood is— No, she's alone. Uh-huh. Uh-huh. Okay." She hung up and smiled at Emily. "She says for you to go..."

Emily didn't wait, just rushed through the doorway and into Wanda's office. The matchmaker looked up from her desk, a broad smile on her face—a smile that quickly faded.

"Oh, dear!" she exclaimed. "Whatever is the matter?"

"Everything's the matter!" Emily felt as if she was

holding herself together by sheer force of will. "Do you know what day today was supposed to be?"

"Uhhh...your birthday?"

"No!" Emily closed her eyes in anguish. "My wedding day."

"That's wonderful!" Wanda beamed. "To think that you and Cody would take my advice and move the wedding up! I'm so flattered."

"Don't be. The wedding's off, my life is off." Emily began to pace. Even the scent of the yellow roses on Wanda's desk failed to calm her this time.

Wanda frowned. "Surely not. Why don't you just sit down and tell me all about it. I'm sure that between the two of us, we can come up with a solution to whatever is troubling you."

"What's troubling me?" Emily ground her teeth together in frustration. "Not a chance. I did a terrible, dishonorable thing—for honorable reasons, you understand. But I didn't tell Cody about it and now he's found out and it's too late."

"Emily, I can't imagine your doing a terrible, dishonorable thing, as you say. You're not that kind of person."

"Apparently I am," Emily said grimly. "I guess you haven't seen it, either, or you wouldn't be so nice to me."

Wanda's eyes widened in alarm. "Seen what?"

"This!" Emily slapped the magazine, permanently creased open to the offending page, down on the desk. "Read it and then tell me that you still think there's hope."

While Wanda pored over the article, Emily stalked

to a window and looked out. The sun was shining and birds were singing. It wasn't fair. There was a blizzard in her heart and it should be reflected in her surroundings.

She couldn't bear to watch disillusionment come over Wanda's face, so she kept her gaze glued to the window. Only at the sound of delighted laughter did she swing around in astonishment.

"How can you laugh?" she demanded.

Wanda stifled giggles. "They all but call me a dotty old lady."

"That doesn't offend you?"

"Why should it? I'm seventy-six, dear—although I'd appreciate it if you'd keep that under your hat. I wouldn't want my fellow employees here at the Yellow Rose to hear that. They think I'm only seventy-three."

"But—but—*dotty*? That means crazy!"

"It also means eccentric, and I don't mind that at all. At my age, who wants to be ordinary?" She closed the magazine with conviction. "No, all in all, I'm not the least bit offended, except..."

"Except?"

"The part about George. Do you really believe George has a bird's nest inside instead of computer guts?"

Emily groaned. "Don't make me answer that."

"I'm afraid I must insist. Because if you think—"

"*I'm going in, Teresa. The Texas Rangers couldn't keep me out!*"

Emily froze, her horrified gaze on the door through which Cody James now barged.

*   *   *

Cody had no idea how he ended up at the Yellow Rose. He only knew that when he saw Emily's compact car parked at the curb, wild horses couldn't have kept him away.

He saw her instantly, standing before a lace-curtained window. Although far from being fashion conscious, he realized at a glance that she was wearing her wedding dress. That knowledge plunged a knife into his heart.

"What are *you* doing here?" they yelled simultaneously.

He followed up that opening gambit. "You didn't wait for me!"

"You picked the time but then you didn't come!"

"I had a flat tire. I did the best I could. You think I didn't *want* to be there?"

"Sorry you missed the chance to tell me to my face what you really think of me?"

She turned her back on him and he saw her shoulders tremble. All at once the anger drained out of him and he felt only relief that he'd found her.

"Emily," he said, "I love you. Please let me explain."

For a minute, he thought she wouldn't respond. Then she turned slowly, her face so vulnerable that it was all he could do not to rush to her.

"*You* want to explain?" Even her voice sounded fragile.

"I meant to tell you," he said. "I swear to God I did. But I loved you so much and we were so happy that I didn't see any reason to take the chance."

She blinked her eyes and shook her head as if clearing away cobwebs. "That's exactly what I wanted to say to you. Cody, I had no idea the story would be so devastating. If I had—"

"Wait a minute." He frowned. "You knew about the story before it was printed? How...?"

She frowned. "Of course I knew. I spied for him. There's no other way to put it, and I'm so sorry. If you'll forgive me, I promise—"

"Forgive you? You've got to forgive me. I know how you feel about guys with money, but honest, it's mostly in land and stock, not cash. Do you think you can get around that?"

"Land and stock?" She caught her breath. "Are you saying you're not a simple cowboy, you're—"

"Half owner of the Flying J, with my brother Ben." His eyes went wide. "And you're saying you spied—"

"For my cousin, a writer for *Boy Howdy!* magazine. I came to the Yellow Rose originally because he wanted a first-person story and he twisted my arm. I had no idea anything so offensive would be printed." She started for Wanda's desk. "I thought you'd seen it, Cody. I thought that was why—"

He caught her halfway and pulled her into his arms. "I don't give a damn what any magazine says. I don't give a damn about *anything* but you." He buried his face in the curve of her shoulder.

She struggled to escape. "But you will. We've got to get it all out in the open or—"

"Children!"

At the command in Wanda's voice, they both snapped to attention.

Wanda sat staring at her computer. "Come quick! George is cranking up."

"Booting," Emily amended.

"Whatever." Wanda gestured frantically. "This doesn't happen all that often. You better get over here before he goes temperamental on us again."

Exchanging puzzled looks, Emily and Cody did as directed. George's screen changed from solid blue to black and white several times, eventually arriving at Wanda's desktop. Without pausing, without direction of any kind from Wanda, the computer zipped past that and into screen-saver mode.

While all three watched in fascination, letters began to scroll across the screen, spelling out, "EMILY LOVES CODY. CODY LOVES EMILY. WHAT'S THE PROBLEM?"

"Yeah," Cody said, his voice husky. "What's the problem, Emily? If you can get over the shock that I've got a couple of bucks, I think I can get over the shock that you spied for your cousin." He raised his brows and fought a grin. "So how stupid did you make me look?"

"Not *that* stupid," Wanda volunteered, adding, "What time is it?"

"Don't know, don't care." Cody put his arms around Emily and she let him—participated, in fact. Holding her close, he drew in a deep breath and realized that her hair smelled like roses.

"Oh, yes, you do," Wanda declared. "Because it's only twenty past two. I'll bet if you hurry, Judge Cooley will still have time to perform a certain wedding ceremony."

Cody went still; in his embrace, Emily did, too. He frowned at Wanda, who looked so innocent he almost expected to see a halo over her head. "How do you know about Judge Cooley?"

She blinked. "Emily must have mentioned the name."

"I'm sure I didn't."

"Then it was a good guess. What difference does it make? Children, children!" Wanda shooed them toward the door. "Hurry! We can't be sure how long the judge will wait."

"Will you come with us, Wanda?" Emily asked.

"I wish I could but I have many more eager singles to transform into happy couples. Perhaps you'll drop by after your honeymoon and we'll drink a toast to a match truly made in heaven."

"You can count on it," Cody said, realizing that the little woman had been right all along. So happy he couldn't stop smiling, he turned to his bride and found that at the moment she seemed to be staring at the single yellow rose on Wanda's desk.

"Take the rose, dear." Wanda handed it to Emily. "There are plenty more where that one came from."

Emily took the rose and waved it gently through the air. Cody caught the rich aroma and sucked in a deep breath.

"Ready?" he asked.

"Oh, yes!"

As they walked through the door arm in arm, he heard Wanda say in a complacent tone, "Well, George, it looks like we've done it again!"

*   *   *

Emily Kirkwood became Mrs. Cody James at seven minutes past four o'clock in the office of Judge Milton Cooley, with Laurie and Mrs. Cooley beaming approval as witnesses. Giddy with a combination of happiness and wonder, Emily clung to Cody with her right hand and to the single yellow rose with her left, trying to concentrate on the words spoken by the judge. Hardly anything registered until she suddenly heard him say, "By the power vested in me by the state of…"

She gasped, her heart soaring. She and Cody had overcome all obstacles and were now man and wife. Turning to her new husband, she looked into his face with all the love and joy her heart could hold. His answering smile dazzled her.

He placed his hands on her waist and hauled her close. "I guess this means you're really my valentine now," he teased, his voice husky.

"I sure am." She slipped her arms around his neck, the rose still dangling from her fingers while a smile tugged at her lips. "And you're mine, Cody James. Wanda's right—we *are* meant for each other."

He threw back his head and laughed, a sound of pure joy. "Honey, from now on, every day's gonna be Valentine's Day!" he promised.

His kiss told her his words were true.

From: MataHari@Upzydazy.com
Sent: February 14, 2:48 p.m.
To: PRKing@SoapCityUSA.com
Subject: All is forgiven.
Very smart, Terry, throwing yourself on my mercy

while I'm on my honeymoon with the most wonderful man in the world. I'd probably forgive Dracula a couple of bites under the circumstances. :-) I'm delighted you got a new job before those clowns at that *Boy Howdy!* rag could fire you. But even if you *are* working in the advertising department for one of the biggest soap makers in the country, I will *not*, repeat *not* be part of any soap test group. Gotta go now—my true love's calling. He asked me to send you a message, but unfortunately I can't repeat it. :-) Hope your Valentine's Day is half as good—make that a quarter as good—as mine! Love ya, Emily James, married lady (Mata Hari no more).

Question: How do you find the sexy cowboy
of your dreams?

Answer: Read on....

Texas Grooms Wanted!
is a brand-new miniseries from

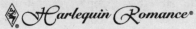 *Harlequin Romance*®

Meet three very special heroines who are all looking for
very special Texas men—their future husbands! Good
men may be hard to find, but these women have experts
on hand. They've all signed up with the Yellow Rose
Matchmakers. The oldest and the best matchmaking service in San Antonio, Texas, the Yellow Rose guarantees
to find any woman her perfect partner....

So for the cutest cowboys in the whole
state of Texas, look out for:

HAND-PICKED HUSBAND
by Heather MacAllister in January 1999

BACHELOR AVAILABLE!
by Ruth Jean Dale in February 1999

THE NINE-DOLLAR DADDY
by Day Leclaire in March 1999

*Only cowboys need
apply...*

Available wherever
Harlequin Romance books
are sold.

Tough, rugged and irresistible...

THE AUSTRALIANS

Stories of romance Australian-style, guaranteed to fulfill that sense of adventure!

This March 1999 look for

Boots in the Bedroom!
by **Alison Kelly**

Parish Dunford lived in his cowboy boots—no one was going to change his independent, masculine ways. Gina, Parish's newest employee, had no intention of trying to do so—she preferred a soft bed to a sleeping bag on the prairie. Yet somehow she couldn't stop thinking of how those boots would look in her bedroom—with Parish still in them....

The Wonder from Down Under: where spirited women win the hearts of Australia's most independent men!

Available March 1999
at your favorite retail outlet.

HARLEQUIN®
Makes any time special ™

Look us up on-line at: http://www.romance.net   PHAUS9

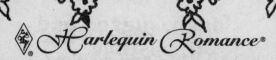

Harlequin Romance®

Rebecca Winters writes wonderful romances that pack an emotional punch you'll never forget. Brimful of brides, babies and bachelors, her new trilogy is no exception.

Meet Annabelle, Gerard and Diana. Annabelle and Gerard are private investigators, Diana, their hardworking assistant. Each of them is about to face a rather different assignment—falling in love!

LOVE
undercover

Their mission was marriage!

Books in this series are:

Available wherever Harlequin books are sold.

HARLEQUIN®

Makes any time special ™

Look us up on-line at: http://www.romance.net

MEN at WORK

All work and no play?
Not these men!

January 1999
SOMETHING WORTH KEEPING by Kathleen Eagle
He worked with iron and steel, and was as wild as the mustangs that were his passion. She was a high-class horse trainer from the East. Was her gentle touch enough to tame his unruly heart?

February 1999
HANDSOME DEVIL by Joan Hohl
His roguish good looks and intelligence drew women like magnets, but Luke Branson was having too much fun to marry again. Then Selena McInnes strolled before him and turned his life upside down!

March 1999
STARK LIGHTNING by Elaine Barbieri
The boss's daughter was ornery, stubborn and off-limits for cowboy Branch Walker! But Valentine was also nearly impossible to resist. Could they negotiate a truce...or a surrender?

Available at your favorite retail outlet!

MEN AT WORK™

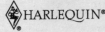 

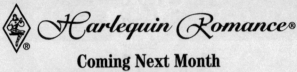

Harlequin Romance®

Coming Next Month

#3543 THE NINE-DOLLAR DADDY Day Leclaire
Ten-year-old Hutch Lonigan had walked into the Yellow Rose Matchmakers Agency with all his savings and demanded the best man he could get for nine dollars! The sleeping partner in the family business, Ty Merrick, hadn't expected that man to be him. But one look at Cassidy Lonigan, and Ty was hearing wedding bells. Only it was going to take more than sweet talk and kisses to persuade young Hutch's stubborn mother to walk up the aisle!

Texas Grooms Wanted!: *Only cowboys need apply!*

#3544 TEMPORARY ENGAGEMENT Jessica Hart
Bubbly Flora Mason had had plans to temp and travel. Her plans had *not* included being engaged to her sexy boss, Matt Davenport. Only, Flora had needed to save face, and Matt had needed a temporary fiancée. So what if they were like chalk and cheese? It was only for two nights. But then, two nights turned into three, then four....

Marrying the Boss: *From boardroom to bride and groom!*

Starting next month look out for a new trilogy by bestselling author Rebecca Winters.

#3545 UNDERCOVER FIANCÉE Rebecca Winters
Annabelle Forrester has only ever loved one man—Rand Dumbarton. The sexy tycoon had swept her off her feet, but their whirlwind engagement had ended bitterly. She hadn't expected to have him walk back into her life and hire her! Only it seemed Rand didn't want Annabelle to work for him...he just wanted her!

Love Undercover: *Their mission was marriage!*

#3546 A DAD FOR DANIEL Janelle Denison
Tyler Whitmore had returned home after nine years to claim his half of the family business. And Brianne was right to be nervous. When Tyler had left he had taken more than her innocence—he had taken her dreams and her heart. But unbeknownst to Tyler, he had given Brianne something in return—her son, Daniel!

BACK TO THE RANCH: *Let Harlequin Romance® take you back to the ranch and show you how the West is won...and wooed!*